Travis tipp
thumb alc

"I know you need more time. I won't push you. But while you're weighing the pros and cons, don't forget to include this in your calculations."

He lowered his head, giving her time to draw back, feeling the jolt when she didn't. At the first brush of his mouth on hers, hunger too long held in check kicked like an afterburner at full thrust. The heat, the fury burned like a blowtorch.

His palm slid to the nape of her neck. His mouth went from gentle to coaxing. From giving to taking. He circled her waist, drew her into him. They were hip to hip, thigh to thigh, her breasts pressed against his chest, her palms easing over his shoulders.

This was what he needed. What he'd ached for. The feel of her. The taste of her.

* * *

Three Coins in the Fountain:
When you wish upon your heart...

Dear Reader,

Are you addicted to chick flicks? I am. I can't count the number of times I've watched *Sleepless in Seattle*, *Notting Hill*, *While You Were Sleeping*, *Pretty Woman* and dozens more I could name. I love the classics, too, both the originals and the remakes: *It Happened One Night*, *Sabrina* and one of my all-time faves, *Three Coins in the Fountain*.

So of course, whenever I'm in Rome, I have to toss a coin in the Trevi Fountain. So far, those tosses have worked! My husband and I no sooner get home from one jaunt to Italy than I start planning the next. Like the heroine of this tale, I love researching guidebooks and working out detailed itineraries. And like Kate, I seem to have the best adventures when they're completely *un*planned!

I hope you enjoy my version of *Three Coins in the Fountain*. I hope, too, that your wishes all come true!

All my best,

Merline

"I Do"...Take Two!

Merline Lovelace

HARLEQUIN® SPECIAL EDITION®

Recycling programs
for this product may
not exist in your area.

ISBN-13: 978-0-373-65943-2

"I Do"...Take Two!

Printed in U.S.A.

A career air force officer, **Merline Lovelace** served at bases all over the world. When she hung up her uniform for the last time, she decided to try her hand at storytelling. Since then, more than twelve million copies of her books have been published in over thirty countries. Check her website at merlinelovelace.com or friend Merline on Facebook for news and information about her latest releases.

Visit the Author Profile page at Harlequin.com for more titles.

To my own handsome hero,
who's explored Italy with me from tip to toe.
What great memories we've made, my darling...
with so many more to come!

Chapter One

"C'mon, Kate. We have to do it."

"No, we don't."

Katherine Elizabeth Westbrook—Kate to the two friends tugging her through the crowd lined up at one of Rome's most famous landmarks—dragged her feet. The water spouting from the Trevi Fountain's gloriously baroque sculptures glistened in the late August sunshine, but Kate had no inclination to participate in the time-honored tradition of tossing a coin in the sparkling pool.

"This is too touristy for words."

"No, it's not." Vivacious, auburn-haired Dawn McGill dismissed Kate's protest with an airy wave. "We've talked about doing this for*ever*."

"Remember the first time we watched *Three Coins in the Fountain*?"

That came from Callie Langston, the quiet one of the

unbreakable triumvirate forged more than twenty years ago, when eight-year-old Kate and her family moved to the small town of Easthampton, Massachusetts.

Callie's reminder of that long-ago sleepover won a smile from Kate. "How could I forget?"

They'd been friends for years by then, all three hopeless romantics and avid movie buffs. In that particular all-night extravaganza, they'd devoured pizza and Twinkies and a gallon of triple ripple mocha fudge while bingeing on rented movie classics.

Callie had chosen the 1940 megahit *The Philadelphia Story*, which had the three teens drooling over a debonair Cary Grant. Dawn had opted for Audrey Hepburn and Humphrey Bogart in *Sabrina*, a sparkling romance that provoked laughter and tears and a burning desire to run off to Paris. Kate had gone with the 1954 version of *Three Coins in the Fountain*, starring Dorothy McGuire and a dreamy Louis Jourdan as a playboy Italian prince. The story of three single women finding love and adventure in Rome made all three girls vow that one day they, too, would visit the Eternal City and toss a coin in its famed fountain.

Kate had loved the movie. Then. Back when she was young and naive and stupid enough to believe in happy endings.

"The wish won't come true unless all three of us do it," the irrepressible Dawn insisted.

"That's right," Callie chimed in. "All for one..."

"...and one for all." Kate dredged up another smile. "Okay, okay! Who's got a coin I can bum?"

"Here."

Dawn thrust a euro into her friend's left hand. It was dull and tarnished and banded by a rim of brass. Soon to be replaced, Kate knew from her work at the World Bank, by a newer, shinier model.

Out with the old, in with the new.

Like her life, she thought, although her new was uncertain and her old hurt almost more than she could bear. Her fist closed around the euro while images cut through her mind like shards of jagged glass. Of Travis roaring up to her college dorm on his decrepit but much-loved Harley. Their engagement the day she'd pinned his air force pilot's wings on his uniform. The wedding two years later that Kate and her two friends had planned in such excruciating detail. The much-dreamed-of trip to Italy that she and her husband had been forced to put off repeatedly while he rotated in and out of Afghanistan and Iraq and a dozen other locales he couldn't tell her about.

The irony of it ate at Kate as she remembered the hours she'd spent planning this dream trip. She remembered, too, all the days she'd buried herself in her own work to dull her gnawing worry about her husband. And the long, empty nights she'd tossed and turned and prayed for his safe return from whatever hot spot he'd been sent to this time.

Now here they were. She and Major Travis Westbrook. In Italy! Separated by only a few hours' train ride. The sad part was that Kate hadn't even *known* her soon-to-be ex was operating out of the NATO base near Venice until she'd talked to his mother just before she and Dawn and Callie had left for their Roman Holiday.

Venice might lie only a few hours north of Rome, but the distance between Kate and Travis couldn't be bridged. Not now, not ever. They'd said too many painful good-byes and spent too much time apart. They'd also grown into different people. Travis, according to the Facebook post his wife had obviously *not* been intended to see, more so than her.

"Make a wish," Dawn urged. "Then toss the coin over your shoulder."

"You don't have to make a wish," Callie corrected in her calm way. "It's implicit in the act. Throwing a coin in the fountain means you'll return to Rome someday."

Kate barely heard her two friends. Fist clenched, eyes squeezed shut, she let her subconscious spew out the anger and hurt that came from deep in her gut.

I wish... I wish... Dammit all to hell! I wish the bitch-whore who bragged on Facebook about having an affair with my husband would develop a world-class case of...whatever!

She flung up her arm and let fly. Not even the water gushing through the fountain's many spigots could drown out the loud thunk as the euro bounced off the basin's rim, or the amusement in the deep drawl that sounded from just behind her.

"You never could throw worth a damn, Katydid."

Her arm froze in the middle of its downward arc. Disbelief jolted through her even as something hot and wild balled in her belly. She couldn't move, couldn't breathe. Her frantic gaze shot to her two friends. Dawn's ferocious scowl was as telling as the mask of icy disapproval that dropped instantly over Callie's face. Kate closed her eyes. Sucked in a shuddering breath. Forced herself to turn slowly, deliberately. Her initial reaction to the first sight of her husband in more than four months was purely instinctive. Bunching her fists, she refused to yield to the all-too-familiar worry over the tired lines webbing his hazel eyes. Refused, as well, to let any trace of anger or hurt seep into her voice.

"Hello, Travis. Your mom must have told you that I finally made it to Rome."

"She did."

Those changeable green-brown eyes drifted over her face and lingered on her mouth. For an incredulous moment Kate thought he might actually try to kiss her. Flashing a warning, she took a half step back.

Dawn and Callie must have read the same intent. They moved simultaneously, one to either side of Kate. Travis's glance moved from Dawn's scowl to Callie's set mouth.

Was that regret that flickered across his face? Or a trace of the amused wariness he'd always insisted he had to pull on like a Kevlar vest when confronted by the trio he'd dubbed the Invincibles? The look came and went so quickly, Kate couldn't tell.

"Rome's a big city." She managed to maintain an even tone, but the effort made her throat cramp. "How did you find us?"

The amusement surfaced. No question about it now. And with it came the crooked grin that had curled her toes inside her black suede boots the first time he'd aimed it her way.

Memories slapped at her again. The gray, blustery November day, the cold wind biting at her cheeks, the icicles hanging like frozen tears from the eaves. Kate and Callie and Dawn had bundled up and were just heading out to the mall when Dawn's older brother pulled into the drive. All three girls had gone goggle-eyed when Aaron introduced the roommate he'd brought home for Thanksgiving.

Although Travis's cheery hello had encompassed the three friends equally, he'd soon cut Kate out of the herd. She'd been a sophomore at Boston College at the time, he a senior at the University of Massachusetts in Amherst. All it took was two dates that magical Thanksgiving vacation. Just two. Then she...

"Finding you wasn't hard."

Her husband's reply jerked her back to the here and now.

"You told me often enough that tossing a coin in the Trevi Fountain topped your to-do list for Rome." He hooked a thumb toward a busy café on the other side of the piazza. "So I staked out a table and waited for you to show."

She hadn't told his mom where she was staying. Hadn't told anyone except her assistant, and David knew better than to divulge her itinerary. Kate wasn't that high up the banking world, but she'd negotiated several multibillion-dollar deals and had recently been featured as one of five up-and-comers on a prominent financial website. Common sense—and her bank's director of security—had advised her to maintain a low profile while traveling abroad. Trust Travis to have tracked her down.

"How long have you been waiting?" she asked with reluctant curiosity.

"Since early morning."

Dawn gave a surprised huff. "You anchored a table in this crowded tourist mecca *all day*? That must have cost a few euros."

"Only enough to feed a family of four for a week. But..." His glance swung back to Kate. "It was worth every euro."

Dammit! How did he do it? A grin, a shared glance, and she was almost ready to forget her angry wish of a few moments ago. Almost.

The bitterness that had spawned it came back, leaving a sour taste in her mouth and a ragged hole in her heart. "You wasted your money, Trav. We said all we needed to when we met with the lawyer."

"Not hardly." The smile left his eyes. "I was served with divorce papers the day after I returned from a classified mission. The meeting with the attorney was set for less than a week later."

"At which point you evoked the Soldiers' and Sailors' Civil Relief Act to delay the proceedings for another ninety days!"

"Only because you—"

He broke off and blew out a slow breath. With a nod that encompassed the elbow-to-elbow tourists cocooning them in a bubble of noise and laughter, he tried again.

"Cm'on, Kate. Let me at least buy you a glass of vino. All of you," he added belatedly.

"You bet your booty all of us," Dawn shot back.

"And only if Kate feels inclined to accept your invitation," Callie put in coolly but no less adamantly.

The Invincibles ride again.

Their united front didn't surprise Travis any more than their fierce protectiveness. He'd known from day one that Kate and her two friends were closer than most sisters. Different personalities, different family backgrounds, but so many shared interests and experiences that they could finish each other's sentences.

And as different as they were physically, each one spelled trouble for the male of the species. With her auburn hair, vivacious personality and lush curves, Dawn drew men like a magnet. Callie was quieter, more reserved, the kind of attentive listener who made men think they were a whole lot smarter than they really were.

But it was Kate who'd sparked his interest that snowy

November day. She'd been bundled into a bulky jacket, her brown eyes barely visible above the scarf muffling the lower half of her face, her curly blond hair streaming from a colorful knit stocking cap.

Her lower half hadn't been as bulked up as the upper half. Her snug jeans had given Travis plenty of opportunity to admire world-class legs above calf-high black suede boots, trim hips and a nice little butt. Yet he'd sensed instantly the whole was so much more than the sum of those enticing parts. Maybe it was the intelligence in those cinnamon-brown eyes. Or the smile when she nudged the scarf down with her chin. Or the way she countered Aaron's teasing with a quick quip.

Whatever it was, by the time Travis headed back to UMass, he was halfway in love and all the way in lust. He'd plunged in the rest of the way in the two years that followed, a hectic time crammed with weekend visits to either his campus or hers and shared summer adventures. Then had come USAF officer training school, followed by the thrill of being accepted for flight school. When Kate flew down to pin on his air force pilot's wings, he'd capped the ceremony with an engagement ring. Between her grad school and his follow-on flight training, it had been another two years before he slid the matching diamond-studded wedding band on her finger.

He'd caught the sparkle of that band when she tossed the coin a few minutes ago. The sight had given him a visceral satisfaction that sliced deep. His rational mind understood a wedding band was merely a symbol. A more primal male instinct viewed it as something more primitive, more possessive. Kate of the laughing brown eyes and lively mind was his mate, his woman, the only one he'd ever wanted to share his life with. And knowing she still wore his ring only intensified Travis's determination to see she didn't take it off.

That would take some doing. He couldn't deny their marriage had hit the skids. He knew his frequent deployments had strained it to the breaking point. Knew, too, that he hadn't sent a strong enough *hands off* signal to the young captain who'd mistaken his interest in her career for something a lot more personal. Travis still kicked himself for not handling that situation with more finesse. Especially since she'd reacted to his rejection by putting a fanciful but too-close-to-the-truth post about her involvement with a certain sexy C-130 pilot on Facebook.

He'd had no excuse for letting the captain get so close in the first place. None that Kate had bought, anyway. And it didn't help that his wife's intelligence and quick smile came packaged with a stubborn streak that would make a Kentucky mule look like a wuss in comparison. She took her time and weighed all factors before making a major decision. Once she did, however, that was it. Period. *Finito.* Done.

Not this time, he swore fiercely. Not this time.

Under Massachusetts law, a divorce didn't become final until three months after issuance of a nisi judgment. That gave Travis exactly two weeks to breach the chasm caused by so many separations and one exercise of monumental stupidity. Determined to win back the wife he still ached for, he issued a challenge he knew she wouldn't refuse.

"Too scared to share a bottle of wine, sweetheart?"

"What do you think?"

The disdainful lift of her brows told him she knew exactly what he was doing, but Travis held his ground.

"What I think," he returned, "is that we should get

out of this crowd and enjoy the really excellent chianti I have waiting."

The raised brows came together in a frown. Catching her lower lip between her teeth, Kate debated for several moments before turning to her friends.

"Why don't you two go on to the Piazza Navona? I'll catch up with you there. Or," she amended with a glance at the shadows creeping down the columned facade behind the fountain, "back at the hotel."

"We shouldn't separate," Callie protested. "Rome's a big city, and a woman alone makes a tempting target."

Travis blinked. Damned if the slender brunette hadn't just impugned his manhood, his combat skills and his ability to fend off pickpockets and mashers.

"She won't be alone," he said drily. "And I think I can promise to keep her out of the line of fire."

"Riiiight." The redhead on Kate's other side bristled. "And we all know what your promises are worth, Westbrook."

Jaw locked, he heroically refrained from suggesting that a woman who'd left two grooms stranded at the altar probably shouldn't sling stones. His wife read the signs, though, and hastily intervened.

"It's okay," Kate told her self-appointed guard dogs. "Travis and I can remain civil long enough to share a glass of wine. Maybe. Go on. I'll see you at the hotel."

The still-aggressive Dawn would have argued the issue, but Callie tugged her arm. The redhead settled for giving Travis a final watch-yourself glare before yielding the field.

"Whew," he murmured as the two women wove through the crowd. "Good thing neither of them was armed. I'd be gut shot right now."

"You're not out of danger yet. I haven't had to resort

to any of the lethal moves you taught me to take down an attacker. There's always that first instance, however."

Travis figured this wasn't the time or place to admit those training sessions had generated some of his most erotic memories. He couldn't count the number of times he'd bedded down in yet another godforsaken dump of an airstrip and treated himself to the mental image of his wife in skintight spandex, sweaty and scowling and determined to wrestle him to the mat.

"I'll try not to become your first victim," he said as she started toward the café.

Without thinking, he put a hand to the small of her back to guide her through the milling crowd. As light as it was, the touch stopped Kate in her tracks. He smothered a curse and removed his hand.

"Sorry. Force of habit."

Kate dipped her chin in a curt nod. One she sincerely hoped gave no clue of the wildly contradictory emotions generated by the courteous and once-welcome gesture.

Swallowing hard, she threaded a path through the crowd. His innate courtesy was one of the character traits she'd treasured in her husband. He'd grown up in a grimy Massachusetts mill town still struggling to emerge from its sweatshop past. Yet his fiercely determined mother had managed to blunt the rough edges he'd had to develop to survive in the gang-ridden town. In the process, she'd instilled an almost Victorian set of manners. A full scholarship to UMass followed by his introduction to the hallowed traditions of the air force officer ranks had added more layers of polish.

And there was another irony, Kate mused as her husband held out a chair for her at one of the rickety tables set under a green-and-white-striped awning. The magna cum laude grad and the thoughtful, courteous gentleman seemed to have no problem coexisting with the gladiator honed by street brawls and the brutal training he'd gone through to become a special operations pilot.

The thought spawned another, one that made her chest hurt as she waited for Travis to claim his seat. Loyalty was another character trait she'd always believed went bone-deep in her husband. He was part of an elite cadre chosen to fly the HC-130J, the latest version of the venerable Hercules transport that performed yeoman service in the Vietnam War. Dubbed the Combat King II, this modern-day, technically sophisticated version of the Herc was the only dedicated personnel recovery platform in the air force inventory. That meant it could fly high over extended distances with air-to-air refueling or go in low and slow to drop, land or recover special operations teams.

Most of the Combat King crew members Kate met over the years were too macho to spout platitudes about the brotherhood of arms or the bonds forged by battle. They didn't have to. The racks of ribbons decorating their service uniforms said it for them. Was it that closeness, the exclusivity of the war fighters' world, that had prompted Travis to take such a personal interest in Captain Diane Chamberlain? He swore it was. Swore he'd only intended to mentor the bright young communications officer.

Kate had ached to believe him. If she hadn't been all too aware of the unwritten rule that what happened when deployed, stayed deployed… If his ambitious protégée hadn't included those graphic details in her Facebook post… If Kate and Trav hadn't already drifted so far apart…

And that, she'd admitted—to him and to herself, when she'd worked through the initial anger and hurt—was the real crux of the matter. Their careers had taken them down such different paths. His from a brand-new pilot with shiny wings to a commander of battle-hardened air crews. Hers from a starting job as a foreign accounts manager at a Bank of America branch to the Washington, DC, headquarters of the World Bank.

Now here they were. Four years of tumultuous courtship and five years of marriage later. Near strangers sharing a tiny table in the city they'd always planned to explore together. As Travis tipped wine from the waiting bottle into dark green glasses, Kate let her gaze drift from the gloriously baroque Trevi Fountain to the tall earth-toned hotels and residences ringing the piazza's other three sides.

"I can't believe we're really in Rome," she murmured.

"Took us long enough to get here."

The rueful acknowledgment drew her gaze from the vibrant scene to her husband. She searched his face, seeing again the weariness etched into the white squint lines at the corners of his eyes. Seeing, too, the scatter of silver in the dark chestnut hair he always kept regulation short.

She couldn't help herself. Before she even realized what she was doing, she reached across the tiny table and feathered a finger along his temple. "Is this gray I see?"

"It is. Helluva note when heredity and the job conspire to make you an old man at thirty-two."

Her gaze dropped to the muscled shoulders molded by his blue Oxford shirt. Its open collar showcased the strong column of his neck, the rolled-up sleeves his tanned forearms. Withdrawing her hand, she sat back and accepted the wine he passed her with a reluctant smile.

"You're not totally decrepit yet, Major Westbrook."

"You, either, Ms. Westbrook. Does it violate the ground rules of our truce if I say that you look damned good for a senior investment accounts officer?"

"Make that executive investments accounts officer. I was promoted two months ago."

"Who died?"

The long-standing joke drew a chuckle. It was a more or less accepted axiom in the banking community that a manager only moved up when a superior keeled over at his or her desk.

Thankfully Kate hadn't had to step over any corpses to reach her present position. Her undergraduate degree in business management from Boston College and a master's in international finance and economic policy from Columbia had given her an edge in the race to the top. That and the fact that she'd begun her career at Bank of America. With BOA's diversity of services and global reach, she'd been able to snag positions of increasing responsibility each time Travis transferred to a new base.

"No one that I know of," she answered.

"Good to hear." Mugging an expression of profound relief, he lifted his glass. "Here's to the World Bank's smartest and best-looking executive investments accounts officer."

She clinked her glass to his, surprised and secretly grateful for the easy banter. She still hadn't quite recovered from the shock of his unexpected appearance in Rome. Although...

She swirled the chianti inside her mouth for a moment, ostensibly to savor the rich, robust flavors of blueberry and clove. Not so ostensibly to deliver a swift mental kick.

She should have at least *considered* the possibility Travis would track her down. Especially since they'd planned and canceled a trip to Italy so many times that it, too, became a long-standing joke. Then an annoyance. Then one more casualty of their crumbling marriage.

"So how are you liking Washington?"

She let the wine slide down her throat and answered carefully. "So far, so good."

Long, agonizing hours had gone into her decision to accept the job at the World Bank. Travis had agreed it was a fantastic opportunity, too good to pass up. He'd also acknowledged that they'd put his career ahead of hers up to that point. What neither of them could admit was that her move to DC had signaled the beginning of the end.

Even then they'd tried to make it work. He'd flown in between deployments for short visits. She'd zipped down to Florida for the ceremony awarding him the Silver Star—despite the fact his plane had taken hits from intense antiaircraft fire, Travis and his crew had managed a daring extraction of a navy SEAL team pinned down and about to be overrun. An air force general and a navy admiral had both been present at the ceremony. Each had commented on how proud Kate must be of her husband.

She was! So proud she often choked up when she tried to describe what he did to outsiders. Pride was cold comfort, though, when he grabbed his go kit and took off for another short-notice rotation to Afghanistan or Somalia or some other war-ravaged, disease-stricken area of operations.

Then there were the ops he couldn't tell her about. Highly classified and often even more dangerous. Like, she guessed a moment later, the present one. She got her first clue when he glossed over her question about how long he'd be in Italy.

"We're not sure. Could be another month, could be more. What about you? How long are you staying?"

"I fly home on the twentieth."

He cocked his head. "Two days after our divorce becomes final."

"Dawn and Callie thought it would be easier to... That is, I wanted to..." She played with her glass, swirling the dark red chianti, and dug deep for a smile. "I couldn't think of a better distraction than touring Italy with the two of them."

"How about touring it with me?"

Her hand jerked, almost slopping wine over the edge of the glass. "What?"

"I owe you this trip, Kate. Let me make good on that debt."

"You can't be serious!"

"Yeah, I am."

Stunned, she shook her head. "We're too far down the road, Trav. We can't backtrack now."

"True." He leaned forward into a slanting beam of sunlight, so close and intent she could see the gold flecks in his hazel eyes. "But we *can* take some time to see if there's enough left to try a different track."

"That's crazy. All we'll do is open ourselves up to more hurt when we say goodbye."

"No, Kate, we won't. Despite Dawn's snide comment a few minutes ago, I hold to my word." Reaching across the table, he curled a knuckle under her chin. "When and if we say goodbye, I promise you won't regret this time together."

Chapter Two

"Kate!" Dismay chased across Dawn's expressive face. "Tell me you're not actually going to traipse off with the man!"

"I said I'd consider it."

"But…but…"

"I know," Kate admitted with a grimace. "The whole idea of this trip was to help me remember there's a big, wide world out there that doesn't have to include Travis Westbrook."

"Now you want to narrow it down again?"

"Maybe. For a week. Or not. I don't know."

The less-than-coherent reply had Dawn swiveling on the crimson brocade sofa lavishly trimmed with gold rope. It was one of two plush sofas in the sitting room of their suite at the five-star Rome Cavalieri. A member of the Waldorf chain, the hotel sat perched on fifteen acres of private parkland overlooking the Eternal City.

With its elegant decor, breath-stealing view of St. Peter's Basilica in the near distance and shuttle service to the heart of Rome, the Cavalieri provided a home base of unparalleled luxury and convenience. The stunning vista framed by the doors of their suite's balcony was the last thing on the minds of anyone at the moment, however.

Ignoring the city lights twinkling like fireflies in the purple twilight, Dawn made an urgent appeal. "Talk to her, Callie. Remind her how many times she and Travis tried to bridge the gap. When he was home long enough to do any bridging, that is."

"She doesn't need reminding. She knows the count better than we do. And God knows you and I haven't scored any better in the love-and-marriage game."

Dawn scrunched her nose at the unwelcome reminder while Callie searched their friend's face. "Which way are you leaning? Yea or nay?"

Sighing, Kate unclipped her hair and raked a hand through the sun-streaked blond spirals. She kept intending to get the shoulder-length curls cut, maybe have them tamed into a sleek bob. Another manifestation of the new Kate Westbrook, like the tailored suits she'd invested in for her move to the World Bank and the two-bedroom condo she'd rented in DC.

"I keep swinging back and forth," she admitted. "My head says it would be a monumental mistake. If I think of it in terms of a return on investment, I can't see how a few days together will alter the long-term viability of our marriage. Not unless we introduce some new variables into the equation."

"Forget equations and investment returns," Callie urged. "Don't think like a banker. Think like a wife who has to decide whether she wants to give her husband one last chance. It's that simple."

"No, it isn't! You and Dawn figure into the equation, too. I can't desert you at the very start of our vacation."

"Sure you can. Granted, it won't be anywhere near as much fun without you. I suspect we'll manage to keep ourselves entertained, though."

"But I planned our itinerary in such detail." Of all the iterations of this trip Kate had devised over the years, this was the most elaborate. "I've laid out all the train schedules, subway maps, museum hours, hotel locations."

"Dawn and I are big girls. We can get ourselves from point A to point B. Can't we?"

"I guess."

With that reluctant concession, Dawn shoved off the sofa and skirted a coffee table topped with what seemed like an acre of black marble to plop down beside Kate. Tucking one leg under her, she reached for Kate's hand and threaded their fingers.

"Much as I hate to admit it, Callie's right. Rambling around Italy won't be nearly as much fun without you. But she'll get us where we need to go, and I'll do my damnedest to hook us up with a couple of studly Fabios. So don't factor us into your equation. All you have to do is decide whether you want to give Travis another chance to break your heart."

"Oh, well, when you put it that way..."

"Dawn, for heaven's sake!"

With an exasperated laugh, Callie joined them on the sofa. Wiggling her bottom, she wedged in on Kate's other side and grasped her free hand.

They'd huddled together like this so many times as young girls to watch TV or giggle over the silliness of boys. As teens, to whisper secrets and weave dreams.

As women, to share their joys and heartaches. More heartache in the past few years, it seemed, than joy.

"It sounds to me as though your head and your heart are pulling you in opposite directions," Callie said quietly. "So my advice, girlfriend, is to go with your gut."

When the three women went down to dinner, Travis was seated at a table in the Cavalieri's gorgeously landscaped outdoor restaurant. Hurricane lamps flickered, the tables were draped in snowy linen and tall-stemmed crystal goblets gleamed. The floodlit dome of St. Peter's Basilica looming against a star-studded sky a mile or so away took the setting out of the realm of sophisticated and straight into magical.

Kate suspected her husband would have preferred she deliver her answer to his outrageous proposal in private. Callie and Dawn had made no attempt to conceal their animosity at the Trevi Fountain, and Travis had to know they would be even less thrilled over the possibility Kate might abandon them. No special ops pilot would ever turn tail and run in the face of the enemy, however. Whatever her decision, he would take his licks.

Pushing his chair back, he rose as a hostess escorted the three women to the table. He'd topped his jeans and blue Oxford shirt with the gray suede sport coat that Kate knew packed easily and wore well. All he needed was a salon tan and a leather shoulder satchel slung over the back of his chair to fit right in with the casually sophisticated European males in the restaurant.

Kate, too, had dressed for the occasion in the caramel-colored slacks and matching hip-length jacket she'd bought especially for this trip. Made of a slinky, packable knit, the outfit could be dressed up with the black silk camisole she now wore or down with a cotton tank and chunky wooden necklace. The appreciative gleam in her husband's eyes as he seated her said he approved of her new purchase.

No surprise there, she thought ruefully as he and the hostess seated Callie and Dawn. Travis had pretty much approved of anything and everything Kate pulled on, from cutoffs and baggy T-shirts to tailored business suits to the strapless, backless gown in screaming red she'd bought for one of their formal military functions. He'd approved of that sinful creation even more, she remembered with a jolt low in her belly, when he'd discovered how easy it was to remove.

Oh, God! Burying her suddenly tight fists in her lap, she was asking herself for the twentieth time if she really wanted to put them both through all the hurt again when Travis reclaimed his seat.

"Almost like old times," he said with a cautious smile.

"Which times?" Dawn oozed honey-coated acid. "Before or after you got up close and cuddly with your little captain?"

Callie winced. Kate's nails dug deeper into her palms. Travis folded his elbows on the table and took the knife thrust head-on.

"Okay, I know Kate shared that Facebook business with you two. I'm sure she also shared my pathetic defense. I'll state it once more, for the record. And only once."

His eyes as hard and flat as agates, he held Dawn's glare.

"I *did* spend time with Captain Chamberlain talking goals and career paths. More than I should have, obviously. I did *not*, however, touch, kiss or otherwise indicate I wanted to have sex with her. Nor did I have any idea she'd posted those pictures of me sweaty and stripped to the waist."

Fairness compelled Kate to intervene before blood was spilled. "They were taken during a volleyball match between aircrews. Travis sent me the uncropped versions later, after..."

She lifted a hand, let it drop. No need to bring all the ugliness into this starlit night. She'd got past it. Mostly.

"After the crap hit the fan," he finished when she didn't. "Now do you think you can sheathe your claws long enough for us to have dinner, Dawn?"

"I can try. But I'm not making any promises."

Surprisingly, the snarky reply took some of the stiffness out of his shoulders.

"Actually," he said gruffly, "I asked Kate to let me buy the three of you dinner for a specific purpose. I want to thank you, Dawn. And you, Callie. You stood shoulder to shoulder with her all these months. I'm more grateful than I can say she had you to turn to."

Dawn blinked, and even Callie was surprised into a semithaw. "It hasn't been easy for you, either," she replied. "We know that. And we want you to know we're good with whatever Kate's decided to do for the rest of her stay in Italy."

"Yeah, well, I want to talk about that, too."

Their server arrived at that point to take their drink orders. The women opted for the Italian classic Bellini, Travis for a scotch rocks. He waited for the server to retreat before laying his cards on the table.

"I know I'm putting a major dent in your plans by asking Kate to spend this time with me. I'd like to make up for it by proposing an alternative to your itinerary, too."

Kate had to bite back an instinctive protest. All her

work, all the timetables and reservations and prepaid museum passes stored in her iPhone, appeared to be going up in a puff of smoke right before her eyes.

"As Kate may have mentioned, I'm on temporary assignment to the NATO base up near Venice. I'm working with a project involving several of our closest allies, one of whom is an Italian Special Ops pilot."

"So?"

Dawn wasn't giving an inch. Travis took her belligerence in stride and continued. "So Carlo's family owns a villa in Tuscany. He says it's within easy driving distance of Florence and Siena and on the fast train line to Milan and Venice. He also says the villa is currently vacant but fully staffed. It's yours if you want to make it your home base for the next week or so."

"Sounds wonderful," Dawn admitted, surprised out of her hostility by the generous offer, "but the hotel here in Rome was our big splurge. We can't afford to spring for a fully staffed villa."

Actually, *she* could. Since Kate regularly advised her on various mutual funds and investments, she knew precisely how much her friend raked in each year as a graphic designer for a Fortune 500 health-and-fitness firm in Boston. She might come across as bubbly and carefree, but she was damned good at her job and had invested wisely.

Callie was a different story, however. She'd walked away from her job as a children's ombudsman with the Massachusetts Office of the Child Advocate just weeks before this Roman holiday. After watching how the heartbreak of the cases she had to adjudicate shredded her emotions, both Dawn and Kate had cheered the decision. They'd also offered to pay her share of expenses for the trip, which she'd adamantly refused.

Still, they suspected she'd had to dip into her savings, and neither wanted her to dig deeper.

Then Travis made it clear she wouldn't have to. "Actually, there would be no charge. Carlo commands one of Italy's crack special ops units. He and I took part in a joint mission some months back, and he now thinks he owes me."

"For what?" Dawn wanted to know.

"Nothing worth writing home about."

Although he dodged the question with a careless shrug, a familiar pressure built in Kate's chest. The American media gave scant coverage to forces from other countries engaged in the war on terror, but she knew troops from dozens of different nations were engaged in the life-and-death struggle. They, like Travis and his crews, put their lives on the line every day.

If this Italian major thought her husband owed him, the joint mission they'd participated in had to have been hairy as hell. Kate's chest squeezed again as she tried *not* to imagine the scenario.

Their server arrived at that point with the three Bellinis and a crystal tumbler of scotch. When she'd served the drinks, Travis picked up where he'd left off.

"So what do you think? Want to spend an all-expense-paid week in Tuscany?"

"That depends on what Kate's decided."

Three questioning faces turned her way. She looked at them blankly for a moment while she tried to factor this unexpected bonus for her friends into an equation made even more complicated by the stress of knowing Travis and this Italian commando had shared what she guessed had been a life-and-death situation. Torn, she took Callie's advice and went with her gut.

"I think you should take this guy... What's his name?"

"Carlo."

"I think you should take Carlo up on his offer." Her gaze turned to her husband. "And I'll take you up on yours."

Dinner went reasonably well after that. The tantalizing prospect of a week in a Tuscan villa with a full staff to see to her needs blunted the sharpest edges of Dawn's antagonism. Kate knew the fiery redhead would snatch up the sword again in a heartbeat, though. So would Callie. Kate would have loved them for that no-questions-asked, just-let-us-at-him support even if the three of them weren't already bonded by so many years of BFF-hood. She loved Travis, too, for setting them up so comfortably.

The insidious thought sneaked in before she could block it.

Damn! Had he preplanned this whole maneuver—leveraged whatever debt this guy Carlo owed him to preempt Kate's nagging guilt over abandoning her friends? Was he that focused, that determined to achieve his objective?

Oh, yeah. Absolutely. Major Travis Westbrook never skimmed down a runway and lifted off without extensive preflight planning. Nor would he hesitate to deploy all available countermeasures to deflect or defeat enemy fire. Still, Kate had to admit he'd orchestrated a pretty impressive op plan for separating his primary target from its outer defenses.

Travis texted Carlo between drinks and dinner to let him know Ms. Dawn McGill and Ms. Callie Langston would arrive at his family's villa the day after tomorrow, assuming it was still available. The Italian Air Force officer texted back confirming availability. The same text provided both directions and the code for the front gate.

Travis shot them to Callie's and Dawn's cell phones before the four of them settled in for a truly remarkable meal. Abandoning any inclination to count either carbs or calories, Kate ordered a grilled-peach-and-buffalo-mozzarella salad followed by a main course of lobster ravioli in a sinfully rich cream sauce.

She would have quit at that point if Dawn hadn't talked her into sharing a spun-sugar-and-limoncello confection that depicted an iconic scene from Michelangelo's Sistine Chapel ceiling. She felt almost sacrilegious forking into the portrayal of Adam's hand reaching up to touch God's. After the first taste, though, she and Dawn attacked the edible art with the same fervor as the Visigoths who'd sacked Rome in 410 AD.

It was almost 10:00 p.m. when their server cleared the table and poured the last of the sweet, sparkling *asti spumante* Travis had ordered to accompany dessert. Another countermeasure, Kate guessed, to prevent a final round of hostile fire from either Dawn or Callie. If so, it didn't work.

When Kate indicated she wanted to talk to Travis for a few moments, her friends waged a short but spirited battle to pay for their share of dinner. Defeated, they pushed away from the table. If Travis thought he'd bought a reprieve with the astronomically expensive dinner, he soon learned otherwise. Dawn took only a few steps, turned back and aimed her forefinger like a cocked Beretta.

"Do *not* forget, Westbrook. Callie and I are only a phone call away. All Kate has to do is hit speed dial, and we're there."

"Good to know that hasn't changed in all the years I've known the Invincibles."

His obvious sincerity angled Dawn's chin down a notch. Just one. The mulish set to her mouth, however, suggested she wasn't ready to quit the field until Callie bumped her hip.

"He got the message. Time for us to make an exit."

"I guess I deserved that," Travis commented as the two women wove their way through the candlelit tables.

"Actually, they let you off easy. You don't want to know the various surgical procedures Dawn performed on you in absentia."

"Most, I would guess, done with a rusty pocket-knife."

"In her more generous moments. Other times she went to work with a hacksaw."

"Ouch."

His exaggerated shudder earned him a faint smile. He had to fight the urge to follow it up by reaching across the table and folding her hand in his.

"I meant what I said earlier," he told her instead.

"About?"

"About being grateful to them. They were there for you when you needed them."

When he *couldn't* be.

Facing his wife across the table, Travis acknowledged that he'd abrogated his role as a husband too many times. When the Bank of America promoted Kate in recognition of her adroit handling of foreign investments during the recession that panicked markets around the world, he'd been swatting mosquitoes at a remote airstrip in Kenya. And just months ago, while she'd agonized over whether to accept the offer from the World Bank and move to DC, he'd been freezing his ass off at a classified location he still couldn't talk about. Time now, he vowed silently, to realign his priorities and reclaim a place in her life.

Assuming she would let him. He'd cracked the door open by getting her to spend this time with him, but the determined expression that now settled over her face suggested he'd have his work cut out to push it open all the way.

"What did you want to talk about?" he asked her.

"We need to discuss the ROE."

"Are we speaking your language or mine?"

ROE in her world stood for *return on equity*, a formula that assessed a company's efficiency at generating profits for its stockholders. In his, *ROE* stood for the rules of engagement outlining the type of force that could be employed in various situations.

"In this instance, they represent the same thing. We need a set of parameters that define what we should and shouldn't do during this time together."

Travis didn't much like the sound of that. "I figured we would play it by ear."

"Right. Like you did with the villa? Tell me you just pulled that idea out of the air."

"Okay, I might have scoped out a few possible courses of action…"

"Exactly. And if I remember the principles of war correctly, the purpose of a course of action is to achieve an objective."

She didn't add *at all costs*, but the implication hung heavy on the air. His brows snapping together, Travis shook his head.

"We're not at war, Kate. At least I hope to hell we're not."

"No, we're not. Now. And I want to keep it that way."

"All right," he conceded, not particularly happy with the direction this conversation was taking. "Let's hear your ROE."

She raised a hand and ticked them off with a decisiveness that told him she didn't intend to negotiate. "One, separate bedrooms. Two, we share all expenses. Three, we decide on the itinerary together. Four, no changes unless by mutual consent. Five, no surprises of any size, shape or dimension."

He took a moment. "Okay."

"That was too easy," Kate said, frowning. "What am I missing?"

"Nothing."

"Do you want to add to the list?"

"I think you've covered the essentials."

Her frown deepened. "This won't work if we're not honest with each other, Trav."

"I am being honest. I can live with those ROE. As long as *you* understand I intend to focus most of my energy on number four."

Focus, hell. He intended to use every weapon at his disposal to make it happen.

"That's my sole objective, Katydid. Gaining your consent…to changes in bedrooms, expenses, itinerary and—oh, yeah—our pending divorce."

"Well." She sat back, her brown eyes wide. "That's certainly honest enough."

"Good." He pushed back his chair, figuring he'd better make tracks before she added to their list of rules. "Why don't you text me a proposed itinerary? I'll look at it tonight and we can negotiate if necessary. Just be sure to factor in some driving time. I want you to see Italy the way it should be seen."

"I, uh... Fine."

The blunt declaration left Kate feeling flustered as they crossed the Cavalieri's elegant lobby to the elevators. Travis didn't touch her this time, not even a gentlemanly hand on her elbow, and she was furious with herself for missing that small courtesy. So furious she jabbed the elevator button before she could miss more than his touch. Like the feel of his breath tickling her ear. The whisper of her name when he...

The elevator doors pinged open. Kate almost jumped in with a promise to zap him a proposed agenda within an hour.

Dawn and Callie were still up and open to further discussion on plans for the remainder of their time in Italy. Snatching up her notebook filled with maps and detailed descriptions of major tourist attractions, Kate worked up an alternate itinerary for them based out of the Tuscan villa. Then she went to work on one for her and Travis.

Driving time. He'd said to factor in driving time. So...

Lips pursed, Kate studied her heavily annotated map of Italy. Since driving in Rome was a nightmare, Kate decided she and Travis should depart the city in the morning, tour the countryside and save Rome for the end of the trip...assuming they were still together at that point. The uncertainty of that churned in her belly as she emailed the proposed itinerary to Travis's phone.

He emailed back while she was still studying her map. The flight plan looked good. No negotiations or changes necessary. He'd pick her up at eight thirty.

* * *

Kate fully expected to lie awake the rest of the night riddled by doubts. She slid between the satiny sheets, still mulling over Travis's stated intention to do whatever he could to change her mind about their future. But almost as soon as her head touched the pillow, the combination of rich food, several glasses of wine and mental exhaustion following hours of wildly conflicting emotions put her out.

The alarm she'd set on her iPhone went off at 7:00 a.m., but the happy marimba barely penetrated. Fumbling for the phone, she hit the snooze button. Twice. So when she finally came fully awake, she glanced at the time, let out a yelp and scrambled to get showered, dressed and packed.

Luckily, she'd packed light for the trip. All three of them had. Just one tote and roll-on each. The absence of heavy luggage made traveling so much easier but restricted choices. Kate had opted for two pairs of jeans, one pair of khaki twill slacks, tanks and Ts in various colors, a lightweight cotton sundress, and her slinky, caramel-colored pants and jacket. Since she would spend the day driving, she decided on jeans and a cap-sleeved black T paired with the chunky wooden necklace.

Callie was up when Kate dashed out of her bedroom, but Dawn hadn't seen the light of day yet. Noting the tote and roll-on, Callie smiled.

"No second thoughts?"

"God, yes! Second, third and fourth. But… Well…"

"You don't have to explain. Just keep safe, Kate, and keep us posted on how things go."

"I will."

The doubts hit with a vengeance while she waited in the Cavalieri's lobby. The break with Travis had been

agony enough four months ago. She had to be certifi-
able to court that kind of pain again.

She swiped her palms down the sides of her jeans and
tried to settle her nerves by admiring the magnificent
triptych that dominated the wall above the reception
desk. The Cavalieri's website boasted that it was home
to one of the greatest private collections in the world.
The hotel's art historian even offered private tours of
the old masters, rare tapestries and priceless antiques
that included, among other things, a crib commissioned
by Napoleon for his baby son.

At the moment, Kate was too revved to appreciate
the art displayed in niches and on pedestals. Last night
she'd thought she'd been so precise, so clearheaded and
unemotional by laying out those ground rules. Then
Travis had to turn them—and her—upside down with
his statement of intent.

And that nickname. Katydid. He'd tagged her with
it one hot summer evening when they'd spread a blanket under the stars and listened to the quivering whir of
grasshoppers feasting on fresh-cut grass. Only he could
call her an insect and make it feel like the soft stroke
of a palm against her skin. And only he could blot out
every one of those zillion stars with a single kiss.

Oh, God! What was she doing?

She tightened her grip on the roll-on, almost ready to
scurry back to her room, when she caught a flash from
the corner of one eye. Turning, she spotted her husband
at the wheel of the convertible that pulled up at the front
entrance. It was low, sporty, hibiscus red, and it gleamed
with chrome. It also, she saw when she exited the auto-
matic doors, displayed a distinctive logo on its sloping
hood. Like the bellman and parking attendant, she was

riveted by the medallion depicting a rampant black stallion silhouetted against a field of yellow.

"Is this a Ferrari?"

"It is," Travis confirmed as he waved off the parking attendant who hurried forward. Rounding the hood, he took Kate's case and stashed it in the trunk. "Compliments of Carlo."

"Free use of a villa *and* a Ferrari? He owes you that much?"

"He doesn't owe me anything. He just thinks he does."

Shadowy images of what must have gone down to rack up such a large debt, real or imagined, made Kate swallow. Hard. Trying to blank her mind to the possible circumstances, she folded herself into the cloud-soft black leather of the passenger seat.

"It's got a retractable hardtop," Travis said as he slid behind the wheel. "If the wind is too much, let me know and I'll put it up."

She nodded, still trying to force her thoughts away from downed aircraft and skies ablaze with tracers from enemy fire. Her husband didn't help by sharing a bit of historical trivia.

"Did you know Ferrari derived his logo from the insignia of a World War I Italian ace?"

"Why am I not surprised?" Kate said drily. "The symbol for such a lean, mean muscle machine could only have come from a flier."

"Damn straight." Grinning, Travis keyed the ignition and steered past a parade of taxis waiting to pick up departing guests. "Count Francesco Baracca was cavalry before he took to the air, so he painted a prancing black stallion on the sides of his plane. Baracca racked up so many kills he became a national hero, and when

Ferrari met the count's mother some years later, she suggested he paint the same symbol on his racing car for good luck."

"The ace didn't object to having his personal symbol co-opted?"

"He probably wouldn't have, but we'll never know. He went down in flames just a few months before the end of the war."

Both the dancing stallion and the sleek vehicle it decorated lost their dazzle in Kate's eyes. "Some good-luck charm," she muttered. "I hope your pal Carlo hasn't stenciled it on his plane."

"No, the aircraft in his unit sport their own very distinctive nose art. The wing's name in Italian is the Seventeenth Stormo Incursori, if that gives you any clue."

When she shook her head, his grin widened.

"It translates literally to 'a flock of raiders.' Not so literally to 'watch your asses, bad guys.'"

"Of course it does. Do they fly the K-2, too?"

K-2 was their shorthand for the Combat King II. The latest model of the HC-130 was still relatively new to the USAF inventory and dedicated to special ops.

"They do," Travis confirmed. "Just got 'em in this year. Carlo and his crew were still doing a shakedown when we got tagged for that joint op."

Kate dug in her purse for a fat plastic hair clip, thinking that her husband and his Italian counterpart had forged quite a bond. It might be of recent origin, but it sounded almost as deep and unbreakable as the one between her, Dawn and Callie.

"I'd like to meet this new friend of yours sometime," she commented as she anchored her hair back with the clip.

"I'd like that, too." He cut her a quick glance. "Want

to amend our itinerary to include the base at Aviano? And maybe Venice?"

"I…uh…"

For pity's sake! They hadn't even left the Cavalieri's landscaped grounds and were already making changes to the agenda. But the lure of Venice proved almost as powerful as the desire to meet this new friend of her husband's.

"Okay by me."

"Great."

When they reached the bottom of the long, curving drive, Travis downshifted and hit the brake. His hand rested casually on the Ferrari's burled walnut gearshift knob while its engine purred like a well-fed feline.

"This baby can go from zero to sixty in three-point-five seconds," he confided as they waited for the cross street to clear. "Once we shake free of Rome, we'll open her up."

Chapter Three

Despite the Ferrari's impressive prowess, it took Kate and Travis all day to make what would ordinarily be a three-hour drive from Rome to Florence.

They left the autostrada about two hours north of Rome and made a leisurely side trip through the Chianti region, with several stops to sample wine and olive oil. After a light lunch in the historic center of Siena, they followed a winding country road to the fortified hilltop town of San Gimignano.

Its seven towers dated from the Middle Ages. Square and unyielding, they stood like sentinels against a sky puffy with white clouds. The town center was closed to nonlocal traffic, so they parked in a lot outside the main gate and explored the winding medieval streets on foot. By then it was late afternoon. A creamy gelato carried them until dinner, which they ate in a restaurant built into one of San Gimignano's ancient walls. The

view from the restaurant's terrace of undulating vineyards and red-tiled farms guarded by tall cypresses was
a landscape painter's dream.

They hit the outskirts of Florence as a sky brilliant
with purple and gold and red was darkening into night.
With typical efficiency, Kate had called ahead to change
the reservations she'd previously made at a small boutique hotel perched on a bank of the Arno River just a
short distance from the famous Ponte Vecchio.

She felt pleasantly tired from the long day. Not tired
enough, however, to banish the awkwardness and un-
avoidable hurt of checking into two separate rooms.
She was the one who'd insisted, she reminded herself
fiercely as they took the elevator to the second floor.

Still, she felt as though a fist had locked around her
heart and was squeezing hard when she paused outside
the door to her room. Key in one hand and the handle
of her roller bag in the other, she covered the hurt with
a smile.

"Thanks for today, Trav. I...I had fun."

"Me, too, Katydid."

They'd both been so careful. No casual physical contact, no sensitive subjects, no reminders of how many
times they'd planned this trip. Now all she could think
of was how much she ached to kick off her shoes and
curl up beside him on a comfy sofa to review the day's
adventures.

Her memories of Italy, she realized suddenly, would
always carry this bittersweet flavor. She had to turn
away before the tears prickling her eyes welled up.

"I'm more tired than I realized," she lied, shoving the
key in the lock. "I'll see you in the morning."

When the door closed behind her, Travis stared at

the white-painted wood panel. He was gripping his own key card so fiercely the edges cut into his palm.

He'd known this trip would be hard. Had fully anticipated spending most of the day with his insides balled in a knot. Turned out he'd grossly underestimated the degree of difficulty. It took everything he had to refrain from rapping on that door, folding his wife in his arms and kissing away the sadness that had flickered across her face for the briefest instant.

A low, vicious oath did little to relieve his frustration. Slinging his carryall onto the bed in his room didn't help, either. Not when all he could think about, all he could see, was Kate's long, slender body stretched out on the brocaded coverlet, her skin bathed in moonlight and her eyes languorous after a bout of serious sex.

"Dammit all to hell!"

He stalked to the minibar and ripped the cap off a plastic bottle of scotch. Glass in hand, he stood at the window and gazed unseeing at the floodlit dome of Florence's famous *duomo*, just visible above the jumble of buildings in the heart of the city.

When he headed down to the hotel's breakfast room the next morning, he was feeling the aftereffects of a restless night. Kate was already there, coffee cup in hand and a fistful of brochures fanned on the table in front of her.

Grunting, Travis squinted to block the glare from the picture windows framing the Ponte Vecchio. Despite the early hour, tourists were already streaming onto the medieval stone bridge that spanned the Arno River. The bridge was topped with multistory shops, just as it had been centuries ago, but shopkeepers now hawked gold instead of scalded chickens and haunches of raw meat dangling from iron hooks. Since the bridge no doubt topped Kate's list of must-see sights, Travis gave fervent thanks they wouldn't have to battle with the flies and smells of an open-air market like those he'd visited in Africa and Asia.

She looked up at his approach. The faint shadows under her eyes gave him a small, totally selfish dart of satisfaction. Apparently her night hadn't been any more restful than his.

The rest of her looked good, though. Too good. He pulled out a chair, wondering how the hell he was going to get through another day without dropping a kiss on the soft skin left bare by the honey-colored curls she'd clipped up and off her neck.

"Good morning."

Her polite greeting only increased his irritation. What was he? Some casual acquaintance? His response came out short and a little gruff.

"Mornin'."

"Uh-oh." Cradling her cup in both hands, she eyed him over the rim. "Rough night?"

"I've had better." He debated for a moment and decided there was no point pretending to be noble. "Took a while to get to sleep. The combination of warm scotch and a cold shower finally did the trick."

"Took me a while, too," she admitted with obvious reluctance. She looked down at her half-empty cup, then up again. "Maybe this isn't such a good idea, Trav."

"What?" He helped himself from the carafe on the table. "You? Me? Sleeping in separate beds? Dumbest idea since pet rocks."

She set her cup down with a clink. "What I *meant* was you. Me. Thinking we could patch our marriage together by playing tourist."

"Okay, hang on a sec."

He needed a jolt of caffeine for this. Preferably main-lined straight to a major vein. He settled for taking it hot and black and bitter. Fortified, he met her challenge head-on.

"First, I'm not playing at anything. I'm dead seri-ous. I love you. Always have. Always will. Second, I don't—"

"Wait! Stop! Back up."

The crease that suddenly grooved her brow annoyed him no end.

"Cm'on, Kate. Despite that Facebook stupidity, you know...you *have* to know you're the only woman I've ever wanted to spend my life with."

When the groove dug deeper, the thought Travis had kept buried in the dark recesses of his mind slithered out of its hole like a venomous snake in search of some-thing to feed on.

"Unless..." He reached deep, fought savagely for calm. "Have you found someone else? Someone you want to spend yours with?"

"No! God!"

"You can tell me. I'll understand." His jaw worked. "I won't like it, but I'll understand."

"Oh, for pity's sake! Do you think I'd dump Dawn and Callie and take off with you if I had another man waiting in the wings?"

Breathing deep, he lopped off the snake's head and booted its carcass into the netherworld. "So what's the bottom line here, Kate? Why *did* you dump Callie and Dawn?"

"Bottom line?"

She caught her lower lip between her teeth. He waited, certain the painful honesty he saw in her brown eyes signaled the end. If it did, he swore with a vow that cut sharp and deep, he would back off. Accept the damned divorce. Let her get on with her life.

"I love you, too," she said quietly. "Always have. Always will. But we've both learned the hard way that love isn't always enough. I guess I wanted... I *needed*... one last shot at bridging the gap between what is and what could be."

His chest unfroze. His heart started beating again. His lungs pumped enough air to fuel an instant decision.

"We need to reopen negotiations."

Instantly wary, she held up both palms. "No way. I'm not ready for—"

"The itinerary," he cut in. "Are you up for another side trip?"

"Depends. Where do you want to go?"

"Let me make a call. Then I'll give you the details."

He tossed his napkin on the table and found a quiet corner in the hall outside the breakfast room. Digging his cell phone out of his jeans pocket, he used his thumb to skim his list of contacts and found the one he wanted. A few seconds later, the call went through the international circuits.

"Ellis."

"It's Westbrook."

Brian Ellis was president and CEO of Ellis Aeronautical Systems, the prime contractor on the highly classified modification to the Combat King's avionics that Travis and his Italian counterpart were currently testing. Ellis had flown over to Italy for a progress review and the final test flights.

A former aviator himself, Ellis had struck a chord with both Travis and Carlo. Over beers a few nights ago, he'd let drop that his corporation was in the process of subcontracting with Lockheed for a multinational, multimillion-dollar contract for an upgrade to the jet engine's electronic injection system. He'd also mentioned that he'd scheduled a visit with one of the other major players in the proposed upgrade.

"You still heading down to Modena this afternoon?" he asked Ellis.

"I am. Assuming Mrs. Wells can manage Tommy."

"Oh. Right."

Travis had almost forgotten that Ellis had brought his six-year-old son to Europe. The plan, the CEO had explained drily, was to spend some quality time with his son before school started while exposing him to as much history as his young mind could absorb.

Travis admired the busy executive for wanting to spend time with his son. But he'd had to grin when Ellis confided that the little stinker had already escaped his nanny twice during those hours his father couldn't be with him. The boy knew better than to leave the hotel on his own, his exasperated father related, and he'd wreaked enough havoc within its centuries-old walls to make it questionable whether they'd be allowed back.

"What's your schedule in Modena?" Travis asked.

"The meet and greet at the headquarters is set for one, followed by a tour of their engine manufacturing facility."

"I need ten minutes. How about we catch you before the meet and greet?"

"Who's we?"

He shot a glance through the double doors of the breakfast room. The sunlight pouring through the windows made a golden nimbus of Kate's hair. With her creamy skin and classic features, she could have posed for one of the Renaissance masters whose paintings filled Florence's museums.

Before he could answer, Ellis connected the dots. "You dog! You convinced your wife to take you back?"

"I'm working on it."

"Then by all means, let's get together in Modena."

"Great. See you a little before one."

Pocketing the phone, he strolled back to his curious wife. "If you don't mind putting Florence on hold for another day, there's someone I want you to meet."

"The phantom Carlo?"

"No, a guy named Brian Ellis. He and Carlo and I... Well..."

"I know, I know. You can't talk about it."

"Ellis is visiting the Maserati factory in Modena this afternoon. It's just north of Bologna, about a hundred klicks from here, autostrada all the way. We could get there and back in time to watch the sun set over the Arno."

Kate arched a brow. "First a Ferrari, now a factory full of Maseratis. You're coming up in the world, Westbrook."

"Could be," he muttered under his breath as he reclaimed both his seat and his coffee. "Most definitely could be."

Kate didn't catch the low comment. His mention of Bologna had triggered something in her memory cells. The city hadn't made her must-see list. Not surprising, with everything Rome and Florence and Milan had to offer a first-time visitor, but it might be worth a short visit.

"You order breakfast," she instructed Travis, "while I check out what else there is to see in Bologna and Modena besides Maseratis."

A bunch, she discovered after a quick search on her iPhone. The city of Bologna dated back more than three thousand years. With its central location smack-dab in the middle of the Italian boot, it had survived and flourished under subsequent waves of Etruscans, Celts, Romans and medieval lords.

"Bologna's home to the oldest university in the world," she informed Travis, "founded in 1088."

"Beats UMass by about eight hundred years."

"It's also famous for its arched walkways," she read. "They run for more than thirty-eight kilometers, connecting the largest historical city center in Italy. The porticoes are actually included on the UNESCO World Heritage list of significant historical, cultural or geographical landmarks."

"Who knew?" Travis commented with a grin.

Certainly not Kate. Fascinated, she Googled away while he ordered an omelet for himself, a fresh fruit cup and a toasted bagel for her.

The order stilled her flying fingers. He knew her so well, she thought with a gulp. Her breakfast routine. Her love affair with classical music, which he'd struggled so valiantly—and unsuccessfully—to share. He also sympathized with her ferocious battle to keep the ten pounds she'd gained since their first meeting from inching up to fifteen, twenty. Not that he'd minded the extra padding. That time in Vegas, when he'd peeled off her bra and panties and slicked his tongue over...

Whoa! This wasn't the time *or* the place to think about where his tongue had gone. Heart hammering, Kate went back to working the phone's tiny keyboard.

"Aha!"

"Aha?" Travis echoed, shooting up a brow. "Does that carry the same connotation as 'gadzooks'?"

"I wouldn't know. I don't read comic books, like some people do."

"More than some. Google 'manga' and see how far back that cultural tradition goes."

"Do you want to hear this or not?"

He surrendered gracefully. "Yes, ma'am."

"Bologna is home to Cassa di Molino, one of Italy's largest banks. It was organized back in the 1800s by a commission of wealthy patrons to manage the city's poorhouses. The commission also encouraged better-off citizens to save by offering them a safe place to deposit funds they could draw on in emergencies or old age."

Her fiscal interests fully engaged, Kate skimmed the article describing the minimum deposit—not less than six scudi—and loans tailored to craftsmen and merchants to stimulate the local economy.

"Back then the bank allocated all profits to helping young entrepreneurs, depositors who fell on hard times and women with no dowries."

"I'm guessing it's not as philanthropic these days."

Ignoring the sardonic comment, she worked her thumbs. "And I think… Yes! Here he is, Antonio Gallo. The bank's new president."

She angled the phone to display a photo of a distinguished gentleman with a genial smile and a full head of silver hair.

"I met him at a conference last year. He mentioned then that he was being considered for a senior position. I didn't remember where until just now, when you mentioned Bologna."

"Sounds like a useful contact."

"Very useful."

"Since we're heading in that direction anyway, why

don't you call and see if he's available for a courtesy call?"

She hesitated for only a second or two. She hadn't factored any business calls into her vacation schedule. Then again, neither had she planned a visit to Bologna. As Travis indicated, however, this was too good an opportunity to let slip.

So much for their carefully reconstructed agenda, she thought, as she Googled the number for the headquarters of Cassa di Molino. After speaking to several underlings, she reached Signore Gallo's executive assistant, who advised that his boss's schedule was quite full but a short visit at 11:20 a.m. might be possible if he juggled some other appointments. Could he call Signorina Westbrook back to confirm? And in the interim, perhaps she might email a short bio?

"Certainly."

She gave him her contact information, then zinged off a copy of the bio she kept stored in her iCloud documents file.

"We're tentatively set for eleven twenty. Can we make that?"

He checked his watch. "Shouldn't be a problem if we hit the road within the next half hour."

"I need to change. Can you get my bagel to go?"

"Sure. Or..."

"What?"

"Rather than drive up and back, we could check out here and go on to Venice after our meetings. Stop over in Florence on the return leg."

He was right. It didn't make a lot of sense to drive a hundred kilometers north, come back, then retrace the route a few days later on the way to Venice and Aviano.

Conceding defeat, Kate mentally shredded their much-amended and totally useless itinerary.

"Sounds like a plan," she agreed.

"You go change and pack. I'll get our breakfast to go, throw my stuff together and meet you in the lobby."

Upstairs, she hurriedly sorted through her limited wardrobe. The slinky caramel-colored pantsuit she'd worn for dinner at the Cavalieri was her most viable option. It would do for a business meeting if she dressed it down.

The chunky wooden necklace she'd brought to wear with the cotton tanks and sweaters was a little *too* down, though. What she needed was a scarf, she decided. One that could perform the double duty of adding a touch of sophistication to her wardrobe and keeping her hair from whipping free of the plastic clip during the drive. Remembering the many street vendors she'd seen set up close to the hotel last evening, she shimmied out of her jeans and into the knit slacks.

Signore Gallo's assistant called to confirm the appointment as she was pulling on a pearly tank. Flinging an emergency makeup repair kit into her purse, she hurried down to the lobby. Travis was already there, holding his leather carryall and a cardboard tray with two to-go cups and a bag she assumed contained their breakfast. He was wearing the gray suede sport coat and jeans again but had paired them with a very European-looking black crewneck.

"I need a scarf," she told him a little breathlessly. "I'll duck out and buy one while they're bringing the car around."

Most of the street vendors were still setting up, but she found one vendor who offered quite a selection of scarves. They ran the gamut from a neon yellow square imprinted with a kaleidoscope of the city's most famous landmarks to a red banner featuring a blinged-up version of Michelangelo's *David*. She was tempted, really tempted, but decided against walking into Cassa di Molino sporting a naked, sparkling *David*.

She settled instead for a silky oblong with an ocher-hued palace set amid a garden bursting with spring blooms and moss-covered fountains. The scarf was long enough to wrap securely around her head and neck yet still leave the ends to flutter like colorful wings when they hit the autostrada.

Kate tried to pump Travis for more information about Brian Ellis during the drive, but aside from sharing the interesting fact that the man had brought his young son to Italy, her husband seemed reticent to go into much detail about the reason for this spur-of-the-moment meeting. Shelving her curiosity, she gave herself over to the enjoyment of the sunlit morning and the rolling vista of small towns and hills covered with vineyards.

With step-by-step directions from MapQuest, Travis navigated the narrow, twisting streets of Bologna's historic center and got them to the Cassa di Molino twenty minutes ahead of their appointment. Barely enough time, as it turned out, to find a parking place. Dodging heavy traffic and a web of one-way streets, they completely circled the block before they noticed the *Riservato Mrs. Westbrook* sign. It was right at the entrance to the magnificent pink-and-white marble palazzo that housed the bank.

A receptionist just inside the cavernous lobby called Signore Gallo's assistant. He came down a few moments later and introduced himself as Maximo Salvatore. Kate tried, she really tried, not to gawk as he led them up a grand staircase graced by wrought-iron railings as beautifully crafted as the paintings and statues gracing the upper level.

Proud of both his heritage and his institution, Maximo had to show them a library with an elaborately stuccoed ceiling, several salons hung with portraits and damask tapestries, and the two antique safes that had secured the hard-earned scudi of the bank's first depositors. He was about to usher them into the president's suite of offices when Kate spotted a discreet sign for restrooms.

"I need to make some emergency repairs," she told the two men. "I'll just be a moment."

"But of course," Maximo said courteously. "We shall await you here."

The ladies' room was small but as beautifully decorated as the rest of the bank. It was also occupied by a woman with both palms planted on the marble sink. Her head was bowed, her shoulders shaking.

"Oh!" Kate started to back out. *"Scusi."*

The woman whipped her head around. She was older than Kate by some years, her dark brown hair streaked with gray. Tears spilled from her red-rimmed eyes and left glistening tracks on her cheeks. Kate hesitated, caught between chagrin for invading her privacy and an instinctive urge to offer comfort.

"Can I help you?"

The older woman answered in an obviously embarrassed spate of Italian.

"I'm sorry," Kate responded. "I don't… Uh… *Non parlo italiano.*"

That produced another mortified river of words, accompanied this time by an agitated wiggle of her hands. Kate got the message and said nothing further as the

woman swiped a wet paper towel across her cheeks
and hurried out.

Kate used the facilities, then made the necessary repairs to her own hair and face. She debated mentioning
the brief encounter to Maximo but decided against it.
Women, especially those in the rarefied upper levels of
international banking, had to stick together. Whatever
was troubling the older woman, she obviously hadn't
wanted witnesses to her tears.

Pushing the episode to the back of her mind, Kate
summoned a smile and rejoined the men. Maximo ushered her and Travis through an outer office with five
gilt-edged desks, three of them empty at the moment. It
also boasted an entire wall of portraits of appropriately
somber bankers staring down at them from elaborately
carved frames.

The inner sanctum was paneled in gleaming golden
oak. Tall windows draped in rose-and-gold damask filled
the office with light. The silver-haired gentleman who
rounded a desk the size of a soccer field was every bit
as gracious as Kate remembered from their brief meeting at the conference.

Signore Gallo welcomed her enthusiastically, professed
himself delighted to meet her husband and accepted her
congratulations on his new position as president of the
prestigious bank with a deprecating shrug.

"An honor such as this comes if one survives long
enough in this demanding and so exhausting profession,
yes? As it will to you, Signora Westbrook."

"Perhaps. If *I* survive long enough."

"Of course you will. You are... How do you say it?
A rising star. One had only to read your profile in *Wall
Street Journal* to know you are on your way to the top."

He caught the look of surprise on her husband's face

and lifted a bushy white brow. "Your wife did not tell you she was identified as one of the young superstars, someone to watch in the field of international investments? No, I can see she did not. You should be most proud of her, Major Westbrook."

"I am. More proud than she knows."

"*Bene, bene.* So. You must tell me. Are you in Italy on business or pleasure?"

Travis left it to Kate to answer. "Some of both, actually. My husband is on temporary duty at Aviano Air Base and I, er, flew over for a visit."

She wasn't lying. Not technically. Travis *was* at Aviano, and she *had* flown over for a visit. Just not with him.

"And you came to our beautiful city of Bologna!" Signore Gallo exclaimed in delight. "There is much to see here and much to do."

"Unfortunately, we just have time for a short visit. We're on our way to Modena, then Venice."

A discreet signal from his assistant reminded the genial banker that his time, too, was limited.

Expressing profuse regrets that he had to terminate their visit, Gallo got to his feet. When Kate and Travis rose, as well, the banker took both of her hands in his.

"You must come to visit again, signora. I should very much like to discuss the recent changes to the liquidity index promulgated by the US Securities and Exchange Commission with you."

"I'd like that, too, but…"

"Yes, yes, you are on vacation. I understand, and I don't wish to impose on your precious time. But may I have Maximo call you in a day or two? Perhaps we can arrange something."

Buoyed by the visit and feeling smug after Gallo's

effusive compliments, Kate exchanged air-kisses with
Cassa di Molino's president before preceding Travis and
Maximo out of the sumptuous inner office.

Two steps into the outer office, her startled gaze locked
with that of the well-dressed matron seated behind one of
the desks. The woman gulped and telegraphed an unmistakable appeal from eyes still showing a faint trace of red.

Kate responded to the mute plea with a friendly, im-
personal nod and let Maximo escort her and Travis down
to the lobby. She fully intended to tell her husband about
the brief encounter, but he distracted her with a demand
for more details about this *Wall Street Journal* profile.
That discussion was cut short by the intense concentra-
tion required to exit the city center.

To make matters worse, an accident just a few blocks
from the bank blocked the narrow streets and enveloped
them in a traffic snarl of gargantuan proportions. As
a result, they pulled into the parking lot of Maserati's
gleaming steel-and-glass headquarters in Modena just
minutes before they were supposed to connect with
Brian Ellis.

And five minutes after meeting the supercharged
aerospace executive, the last thing on Kate's mind was a
chance encounter in the ladies' room of Cassa di Molino.

Chapter Four

"You're going to work for Ellis Aeronautical Systems? As VP for test and evaluation?"

Kate's incredulous gaze bounced from her husband to the executive in what she guessed was a two-thousand-dollar suit and back again.

"Starting the first of the year?"

They were ensconced in a small conference room on the top floor of the steel-and-glass tower housing Maserati's headquarters. Its solid wall of windows overlooked the curving, glass-fronted building that showcased the world-famous manufacturer's latest automotive offerings.

Sunlight slanted through the windows' mini-blinds and painted Travis's face in alternating stripes of shadow and sincerity as he responded to her shocked question. "It isn't a done deal yet."

"Not from lack of trying on my part," Ellis admitted with a wry smile.

He was a big man. Not heavy, but tall and broad shouldered, with ice-blue eyes above a nose that sported a slight dent in the bridge.

"Your husband's a legend among the special ops community, Ms. Westbrook. Not just because of the rows of ribbons on his dress uniform. They speak to his airmanship and courage under fire. Add in his hours in the cockpit, and we're talking a level of experience few can match. I know I don't have to tell you he's racked up twice as many combat hours as other C-130 pilots with his years in service."

"No," Kate agreed tightly, "you don't. But..."

She swiveled her ultramodern chrome-and-leather sling chair to face her husband. Now that her first stunned surprise had ebbed, other emotions flooded in. Chief among them was doubt that he could jettison a career he loved without a mountain of regret. And guilt that he would even consider it. And a sudden, swamping hope they might carve out a future together after all. Those jumbled emotions were followed almost instantly by a spurt of indignation that he would spring this on her here, in front of a total stranger, with no warning.

"How long have you been considering this?" she asked with an edge to her voice.

"Brian made the offer a few days ago, but I didn't even consider taking him up on it until last night."

When they'd adjourned to separate bedrooms. He didn't say it. He didn't have to. Kate could fill in the blanks.

"And before I do accept it," he said instead, "I want you to hear exactly what the offer entails."

Ellis's keen blue eyes assessed Kate's face. "We

usually try to woo the spouse as well as a prospective executive-level hire, Ms. Westbrook. We recognize a position like this is a team effort. If we were meeting at our corporate headquarters, we'd do this more graciously."

"Call me Kate. And I don't need to be wooed with expensive dinners and visits to corporate headquarters."

"Then I'll skip the hype and cut straight to the basics."

Any other time she would have admired the polished manner so at odds with those wrestler's shoulders. Now all she could think about was the fact that Travis was actually considering turning his whole world around. *Their* whole world.

"We're a Fortune 500 company specializing in the research, design and manufacture of advanced aircraft avionics. About half our contracts are with the Department of Defense, the rest with other agencies in the States and abroad. Our headquarters are in Bethesda, Maryland, which is convenient, considering our primary interface is with Lockheed and Northrop Grumman, both located nearby."

Kate's heart gave a little bump. Bethesda was only thirty minutes from where she worked in downtown DC.

"Our main manufacturing and test facility is in Texas. As VP for test and evaluation, Travis would have to spend a fair amount of time there and at the plants of our various subcontractors."

Last Kate had heard, there were no land mines and IEDs blowing off limbs in Texas. No rocket-propelled grenades slamming into communications centers and crew quarters. No surface-to-air missiles arcing through the sky to take out low-flying aircraft. Every third

Texan might tote a gun, but most of them weren't out to kill men and women wearing a uniform with a US flag.

"Your husband and I are still negotiating a total salary and benefits package," Ellis told her, "but I realize it'll have to be sweet to entice him to leave the military at this midpoint in his career. Big decision, I know."

"Very big," she echoed, still trying to take this all in.

"Given your financial background, I'm not surprised he wants your input before we finalize any deal." His smile suggested that he anticipated some spirited salary negotiations. "That's about as basic as I can get. Do you have any questions for me?"

"Dozens," she admitted, "but none that need asking until I talk to Travis."

"Understood. Well, I'd better head to my meeting." When they got to their feet, Ellis enfolded her hand in his. "It's good to meet you, Kate. I've heard a lot about you."

She certainly couldn't say the same.

"Travis mentioned he was going to try and entice you up for a visit to the base at Aviano," the executive said. "Maybe I'll see you there or at the hotel in Venice. Although," he added, his smile turning rueful, "I'd better warn you that I come prepackaged with a hyperactive six-year-old. He's already tumbled into the Grand Canal once. I'd like to believe that'll be his only swim, but I'm not putting any money on it. Or that he won't take some unsuspecting bystander with him."

She had to laugh at his sardonic expression and couldn't help thinking that he and Travis would be a good fit. They were both so down-to-earth, yet supremely confident in themselves and their abilities. When Ellis departed, however, the look she turned on her husband wasn't exactly complimentary.

Folding her arms, she skewered him with an ice-pick stare. "Why in hell did you let me walk into this cold?"

"Two reasons. First, I wanted your no-frills, no-holds-barred gut reaction."

"Oh, you'll get that."

"Second…"

She waited, foot tapping, until he finished more slowly.

"I guess I needed to hear the offer again before I let myself believe it might happen."

She dropped her arms, her throat suddenly tight. "Do you *want* it to happen, Trav?"

"Only if you do."

The answer cut straight to the tangled knot of their marriage. Kate had always known he'd quit the service in a heartbeat if she asked him to. For that reason, she *couldn't* ask him to.

"We were at the bar in the hotel," he related. "Brian and Carlo and me. The project we're working on passed a major milestone earlier that day and we were having a few beers to celebrate. Brian let drop that the executive who runs his test-and-evaluation division is retiring and asked if I knew anyone with my kind of expertise and number of hours in the cockpit to replace him. I don't know who was more shocked—him, Carlo or me—when I said I might be interested in the job."

Travis had heard the words come out of his mouth and been as stunned as the two men he'd come to know so well in recent weeks. Yet as soon as his brain had processed the audio signals, he'd recognized their unshakable truth. If trading his air force flight suit for one with an EAS patch on it would win Kate back, he'd make the change today.

"So what do you think?" he asked her. "Again, your first, no-frills, no-holds-barred gut reaction?"

"I won't lie," she admitted slowly, reluctantly. "My head, my heart, my gut all leaped for joy."

He started for her, elation pumping through his veins. The hand she slapped against his chest to stop him made only a tiny dent in his fierce joy.

"Wait, Trav! This is too big a decision to make without talking it over. Let's...let's use this time together to make sure it's what you really want."

"I'm sure. Now."

"Well, I'm not." Her brown eyes showed an agony of doubt. "The military's been your whole life up to now."

"Wrong." He laid his hand over hers, felt the warmth of her palm against his sternum. "You came first, Katy-did. Before the uniform, before the wings, before the head rush and stomach-twisting responsibilities of being part of a crew. I let those get in the way the past few years. That won't happen again."

The doubt was still there in her eyes, swimming in a pool of indecision. He needed to back off, Travis conceded. Give her a few days to accept what was now a done deal in his mind.

"Okay," he said with a sense of rightness he hadn't felt in longer than he could remember, "we'll head up to Venice. Let Ellis's proposal percolate for a day or two."

And then, he vowed, they would conduct a virtual burning of the divorce decree before he took his wife to bed.

They left the Ferrari in a patrolled section of the parking garage on Tronchetto Island and took a water taxi across the broad, slate-gray waters of the bay. The wind whipped Kate's hair free of both her clip and colorful head scarf. She didn't even notice as the vaporetto skimmed the choppy waters.

The driver throttled back to enter the Grand Canal. Venice's busy central waterway hummed with water taxis, gondolas filled with tourists snapping picture after picture, and the flat-bottomed scows that transported goods throughout the city. Kate stood braced against the vaporetto's deck, her upper body exposed by its open hatch, her face alive with the delight of viewing one of the world's great treasures for the first time.

Travis had driven up and back from Aviano often enough to take the distinctive fusion of Byzantine, Moorish and Roman architecture in stride. Viewing it through his wife's eyes, though, gave him a renewed appreciation of the arched bridges, domed churches and tall, narrow houses with laundry strung across their windows.

As they curved past the Grand Canal's first bend and headed for the Rialto Bridge, the houses became wider, grander…including the one the vaporetto driver nosed up to. Painted a deep terra-cotta red, it boasted a colonnade of white marble pillars topped by three stories of intricately arched windows.

"This is our hotel?" Kate asked, her eyes wide as Travis helped her out of the boat and onto a marble landing slick with water that lapped from the canal.

"It is."

"Travis!" Her gaze roamed the fifteenth-century exterior. "This has got to cost a fortune!"

"Not as much as it would have if Carlo didn't have an in with the owner. I think they're cousins or something."

"Wow," she murmured as the vaporetto driver handed up their cases. "Your friend and his family certainly live well."

"So it would seem. I don't know the whole story,

though. Carlo doesn't talk about his background, and I'm not about to pry. All I know is that he prefers his air force rank of *maggiore* to the one he inherited."

"Which is?"

"Prince of Lombard and Marino."

"What?" Disbelief and incredulity chased across her expressive face. "Have you stumbled into some alternate universe? One populated with Ferraris and Maseratis, Italian princes and CEOs of Fortune 500 companies?"

"I've asked myself that same question the past few weeks," Travis admitted as a uniformed bellman popped out of a door at the rear of the landing.

"Buonasera. Benvenuti a Palazzo Alleghri.*"*

"Thanks."

Switching seamlessly to English, the bellman gestured to a marble staircase. "The lobby is just up those stairs, signore. If you will check in, I'll have your bags carried to your room."

The stairs led to a black-and-white-tiled loggia dominated by gilt-edged mirrors, six-foot-tall vases bursting with flowers and a statue of a muscular Roman goddess in flowing marble robes.

"Ah, yes," the receptionist said when Travis gave his name and a credit card. "Maggiore *e* Signora Westbrook. As *il principe* requested, we've put you in the blue suite. I think you will find it very comfortable."

Comfortable didn't come close to describing the luxurious set of rooms. The source of the suite's name was immediately apparent in the shimmering ultramarine brocade drapes in the sitting room. The same fabric covered the upholstered chairs and was picked up in the broad stripes of an Empire-style sofa with one rolled arm and gleaming gilt trim. A Murano glass chandelier in a rainbow of colors hung from an elaborately carved ceiling medallion, and the antique marble-topped bombé chest that served as a sideboard could have graced a medieval prince's palace.

Which it probably had, Kate thought as she paused in the arched entry to the bedroom to gape at its opulence. More rich brocade, more handblown glass, more sumptuously carved plasterwork...and a massive bed of silver-painted wood with four flat-topped posts entwined in gold-leaf vines. She was still taking in the suite's splendor when the bellman arrived with their luggage. He placed their two small pieces on the bench at the foot of the bed before turning to ask if they cared to dine on the rooftop terrace.

"The view is one such as you will see nowhere else."

Kate looked to Travis, who endorsed the recommendation. "He's right. Once you see Venice in the moonlight, you'll forget that coin you tossed in the Trevi Fountain and always come back here instead of Rome."

"You think?"

"I know."

"Then the terrace it is."

"*Bene.* What time shall I tell the concierge to reserve your table?"

Since they'd eaten breakfast on the run and skipped lunch, they opted for an early dinner.

"I shall see to it."

Silence descended after the bellman's departure. Travis lingered at the foot of the bed; Kate stood by the windows. Her hair was a wind-tossed tangle from the drive and vaporetto ride. Her expression reflected none of the enchantment she'd displayed earlier.

He had a good idea why and gestured to the four-poster. "Sorry about the one bed. I can bunk on the sofa in the other room."

She nodded, but the troubled look didn't leave her eyes.

"We don't have to stay here, Kate. Or in Venice, for that matter. Aviano's only an hour away. My hotel outside the base doesn't have anywhere near the view or elegance, but..."

"It's not the palazzo." She carved a vague circle in the air. "It's everything. This trip. Ellis. His job offer. Your prince. Us. I feel as though I've jumped on a speeding train and don't have a clue where it's heading."

"And that's bad?"

"Unsettling."

Good, Travis thought fiercely. Unsettled was good. He'd take uncertainty any day over her previous insistence they'd grown too far apart to find their way back. And just to inject a little more doubt...

He crossed the room and brushed a knuckle down her cheek. Her eyes widened, but she didn't flinch, didn't draw back.

"Maybe our approach to life was too deliberate the first time around, Katydid. Looking back, we laid it out like a playbook. You would finish your undergraduate degree. I would go through flight school. We'd get engaged, get married, work our way up the chain, take on more challenges, more responsibilities. Start a family only when we were ready."

"That *was* the plan," she agreed, sighing as he made another light pass over her cheek. "What we didn't take into account was how those challenges and responsibilities would force us into such separate worlds. You gone so much, me turning more and more to work to fill the void."

She hesitated but had to tackle the subject that had become increasingly painful for them both. "It wouldn't have been smart or right or fair to bring a baby into that void and expect him or her to fill it."

"So we throw that plan out the window," Travis said with rigidly subdued violence. "Start new. Here. Now. That's why I wanted you to meet Ellis. Why I'm ready to hand in my papers as soon as I return to the base and complete this project." He tipped her chin up, drew his thumb along her lower lip. "I know you need more time. I won't push you. But while you're weighing the pros and cons, don't forget to include this in your calculations."

He lowered his head, giving her time to draw back, feeling the jolt when she didn't. At the first brush of his mouth on hers, hunger too long held in check kicked like an afterburner at full thrust. The heat, the fury burned like a blowtorch.

His palm slid to her nape. His mouth went from gentle to coaxing. From giving to taking. He circled her waist, drew her into him. They were hip to hip, thigh to thigh, her breasts pressed against his chest, her palms easing over his shoulders.

This was what he needed. What he'd ached for. The feel of her. The taste of her. The pleasure was sharp, knifing and so welcome he had to tap his last reserve of willpower before he could raise his head.

When her lids lifted, the smoky desire in her eyes almost snapped his last thread of restraint. He was a breath away from scooping her up and depositing her on that shimmering blue bedspread when she huffed out a husky laugh.

"Well, looks like there's one aspect of our relationship we won't have to restart."

"You sure?" He waggled his brows. "That was a pretty small sample. Maybe we should run another test."

Her laugh was more natural this time, although she didn't quite meet his eyes as she eased out of his arms.

"No time for another test if we're going to make an early dinner. As much as I enjoy swanking around in a Ferrari convertible, I need to soak the road and wind out of my pores. It may take a while," she warned. "Do you want the shower first?"

"You go ahead." He paused for a beat. "Give a shout if you need me to scrub your back. I'm pretty good at it, if you recall."

He was, Kate admitted as she dug out her cosmetic case and clean underwear. Very good! Really excellent, in fact, at scrubbing her back, her front and everywhere in between. They must have slopped an ocean of soapy water onto the tiles in the bathroom of their first apartment.

The erotic mental image took on a more vivid texture with her nerves still skittering from the feel of his mouth and body against hers. Just the sight of the clawfoot tub set in solitary splendor on a raised dais brought the heat rushing back. She sat on the tub's edge, set the old-fashioned black plug and twirled the gilt-edged taps. Steam rose almost instantly from the gushing spout, as hot and vaporous as Kate's memories.

It was only after she'd added floral-scented bath salts and adjusted the temperature that all-too-familiar guilt edged out the memories. Guilt that her pride in her husband's service to his country didn't compensate for empty days and lonely nights. Guilt that she couldn't adjust to the long rotations and short-notice deployments with the same seeming ease as other wives in his unit. Guilt that her gnawing loneliness only added to the stress Travis carried into every op.

Now he was ready to leave the military. Walk away

from a job he loved and the comrades in arms who understood the dangers and frustrations and challenges he faced every day. The men and women who spoke the same language and shared the same highs and lows.

As Kate stripped down and slid into the frothy bubbles, her rational self reared up to do battle with the ever-present guilt. Theirs wasn't the only marriage to crack under the pressure. The divorce rate in the air force was the highest in more than two decades. It ran even higher for special ops. Separations, stress and the high risk of the job all took their toll.

And dammit, she shouldn't feel so guilty at the prospect of Travis walking away from that close-knit special ops community. Judging by the interaction between him and Brian Ellis earlier this afternoon, her husband might well find the same satisfaction, the same camaraderie, outside the military as he did in it.

Buoyed by the thought, she grabbed the puffy sponge supplied by the hotel and dunked it in the still-fragrant froth. A thorough scrubbing left her skin tingling and her thoughts free to dwell on something other than the guilt she'd carried for so long.

Like the kiss Travis had laid on her a few moments ago. And the feel of his shoulders bunching under her palms. And her almost suffocating need to glide her palms over that smooth, hard muscle again. Tonight. After a candlelit dinner on the terrace, with the grand palazzi and glistening canals of Venice.

Oh, hell! Who needs candlelight and canals?

Travis was willing to risk all to save their marriage. Could she do any less?

The decision came without conscious thought, so sudden and sure it brought her out of the tub draped in a slick sheen of bubbles. Plucking a towel from the rack, she wrapped it around her. With only a fleeting prayer of thanks that she'd continued on the pill, she left a trail of wet footprints all the way through the bedroom.

Travis was in the sitting room, his shoes kicked off and ankles crossed on a hassock as he surfed channels on the sixty-inch flat-screen TV. Kate caught snippets of Italian, German and Japanese before she cleared her throat.

The ostentatious "ahem" brought his head around. The sight of her towel-draped body froze his thumb on the remote. The channel stuck on an Asian newscaster with a mellifluous voice describing what looked like a typhoon forming in the South Pacific. The swirling turbulence on-screen matched the chaotic thump of Kate's heart.

"You were right," she said, her pulse pounding.

The remote hovered midair. Caution threaded his voice. "About?"

"The sample was too small. We should run another test."

She almost laughed at his look of blank confusion. It took him a few seconds to make the connection to their kiss right before she'd retreated to the bathroom.

Then his feet hit the floor, the remote hit the hassock and he was out of the chair in one fluid move.

Chapter Five

Travis had vowed to give Kate the romantic Italian interlude she'd always dreamed of. He'd constructed contingency plans for every possible variation, from exploring the hustle and history of Rome to roaming sun-kissed Tuscan vineyards to braving Naples's teeming streets and feasting on the city's famous margherita pizza. Each contingency included the admittedly tenuous hope that they would make slow, delicious love every night they were together.

Slow and delicious didn't so much as pop into his head as he came out of his chair. All he could think of, all he could focus on, was his near-naked wife. The sheen of damp flesh above and below her towel sent his self-control into a frantic free fall. Her wet hair made him hurt with the need to bury his fists and his face in the tangled, silky mass. He was across the room in two strides. Had her backed against the wall in two more.

"I don't know what size sample you had in mind," he got out in a low growl, "but I suggest we start here."

His mouth covered hers, hard and hungry. When he moved to her throat and nipped at the taut cords, his blood was hammering like a pile driver. He inhaled the scent clinging to her wet skin while he feasted on her.

"Then we'll work down to here..."

He tugged the towel free, let it drop in a soggy pile at their feet. Cupping her breast, he teased the nipple with his thumb until it stiffened, then dipped to take the dusky peak in his mouth.

"Oh, Travis." Kate's spine arched. Her fingers dug into his shoulders. "It's been so long."

He grunted a fervent agreement and shifted his attention to her other breast. Head back, neck arched, she let him take his fill until her skin flushed and her breath came in short pants. Wedging an elbow against his chest, she pushed him back a few inches. His heart damned near stopped until she gasped out an urgent demand.

"You need...to get out...of those clothes."

He didn't make it all the way to naked. Her feverish hands shoved down his jeans and shorts, but he barely got one leg free before she wrapped a fist around his already rampant sex. Her fingers were hot, tight, eager. His were every bit as greedy, parting her thighs, exploring her slick folds, matching her stroke for stroke until her brown eyes went wild and stormy.

"Now, Trav. Now!"

He didn't need any further urging. Cupping her bottom, he raised her a few inches, bent a knee and positioned himself. Some last shred of sanity screamed at him to ease in. Slowly. Slowly. Wait for her to open. Take him in. Bring him home.

Every muscle in his body quivered, every tendon strained. Then she hooked a calf around his thigh and ground her hips down on his. Somehow he managed to hang on long enough to pull out, thrust in. Then he shot her into the stratosphere with him.

Kate wasn't sure what pierced her haze of sensual delight. Her first guess was the scratchy itch of textured plaster against her butt. Then again, it might have been the bony hips pinning hers to the wall or the hard chest mashing her breasts. One thing about Travis Westbrook, she thought ruefully as the last waves of pleasure dissipated. There wasn't an ounce of soft or cushiony anywhere on the man.

He'd dropped his forehead to hers. Another pressure point. She tried to adjust by angling her head and body a few degrees. The wiggle only dug his hips deeper into hers. He was still inside her, she realized belatedly, although how long that condition would last was questionable.

"Travis."

"Unnngh."

"I'm going to have permanent marks on my back and butt."

His head lifted. "Huh?"

"My butt. My back. The wall."

"Oh." His hazel eyes went from semidazed to almost clear. "Right."

He eased away a few inches, taking her with him, and hefted her higher while somehow managing to kick free of the jeans still tangled around one foot. She swung up her right leg and caught her left to form a tight vise around his waist as he started for the bedroom. She clung to him, breathing in the sharp tang of his skin.

The scent of him, the feel of him against her, rekindled her sluggish senses. By the time they reached the bed, she'd come alive again. Travis, however, barely got the bolster yanked down and Kate deposited on the sheets before he shed his shirt and shoes and collapsed in a boneless heap beside her. He lay sprawled on his back, long limbed and loose and wearing an expression she could only describe as goofy.

Kate rolled onto her side and propped up on an elbow. As though it had a will of its own, her hand touched and explored and revived memories she'd tried so hard to suppress. The smooth curve of his shoulders, the barrel of his ribs, the ropy muscles of his thighs were as familiar as the nicks and dents he'd collected during a very active boyhood and vigorous manhood.

He'd added a new one, she saw with a hollow sensation in the pit of her stomach. As she feathered a fingertip over the still-angry scar on his hip, the old fear grabbed her by the throat. She had to swallow hard before she could ask.

"How did you get this?"

He didn't open his eyes or alter his lazy sprawl. "Lousy intel."

"I need more than that."

"We flew into a forward airstrip that wasn't as secure as the locals swore it was. Rebels overran the field, and we had to get out of Dodge in a hurry." He pried up one eyelid and angled a look at his hip. The chagrin in his voice tipped into disgust. "It was only a flesh wound, not much worse than a mosquito bite, but I bled all over the damned cockpit before we got back in the air."

She felt caught in the vise of her worst nightmare. She'd dreamed it so many times, with so many variations, and always in terrifying Technicolor. Perimeter forces under assault and falling back. Armed rebels swarming some unimproved dirt landing strip. Travis and his crew scrambling aboard, engines roaring to full power, props spitting up clouds of dust, bullets pinging off the fuselage.

She wanted him out of that. So badly *she* hurt with it. But not unless he wanted it, too. She pushed up higher, her voice suddenly tight and urgent.

"Be honest with me, Trav. Would you really be happy working with Brian Ellis?"

He rolled onto a hip. He had both eyes open now. She saw the light from the windows reflected in their dark pupils, and absolute certainty in their hazel depths.

"Yes, Katydid, I would."

"Then do it. Accept the offer. For me. *Please.*"

He didn't blink, didn't question her abrupt change of mind and didn't hesitate. "Consider it accepted."

With a small sob, she fell forward and buried her face in the warm skin of his neck. Joy flooded her, riding a crest of sheer relief. A distant corner of her mind warned that guilt would return later, but at that moment her heart had no room for anything but happiness.

"I'll call Brian tomorrow. And Colonel Hamilton," he added. "I'd better tell the old man personally before he gets word via the grapevine."

"Yeah, you'd better."

Kate had got to know the colonel and his wife, socially and otherwise. Carol Hamilton served as mentor and confidante to spouses who faced the challenge of coping with sick kids and lost dogs and the frequent short-notice deployments of their husbands and wives. The vivacious brunette took those responsibilities as seriously as her husband did his.

Although Colonel Hamilton would probably cut off

his right arm before admitting to any favorites, Kate knew he considered Travis one of the best and brightest officers in his command. He would *not* be happy to hear Major Westbrook had decided to hang up his air force uniform.

Travis didn't seem particularly daunted at the prospect. His shoulder muscles bunching under Kate's cheek, he slid a hand through her hair and tipped her head back.

"I'll put in the official request for separation from the air force as soon as I get back to Aviano. But not for you, Kate. For us."

When he lowered his head, his kiss smothered the doubt and loneliness and worry she'd lived with for so long. She knew flying was in his blood. Knew he would still strap himself into a cockpit and probably court more than his share of risks as Ellis Aeronautical Systems' VP for test operations. But he wouldn't be dodging surface-to-air missiles or taking off in a hail of bullets.

Or would he?

She jerked her head back, her eyes wide with dismay. His filled with instant wariness.

"What?"

"This big modification you said EAS was working on with Lockheed. Will it require flying into hostile airspace to test it?"

"Maybe. I can't talk specifics at this point. I'm not cleared into the program and don't know anything about it."

"Okay. All right." She chewed the inside of her cheek and fought for calm. "Here's the deal. I need to know what EAS's VP for test and evaluation does. Specifically. I want statistics. Probabilities, if you can't give me hard data. Or at least an estimate of the risk factors involved in testing the kind of aeronautical equipment EAS develops."

He didn't pretend to misunderstand where she was going but did his best to deflect her aim. "For God's sake, Kate. I'll be overseeing a small army of engineers, test pilots, mechanics and technicians. If I log enough hours in the air every month to maintain my FAA certification, it'll be a miracle."

"I don't care," she said stubbornly. "I want to crunch the numbers. And don't hand me the usual BS about the data being classified."

She expected him to protest that it wasn't bull. She didn't expect him to burst out laughing.

"I don't see what's so amusing."

"You don't, huh?"

Still laughing, he took her with him as he fell back on the sheets. They landed in a tangle of arms and legs, chins bumping.

"How about the fact that we're naked and in bed together for the first time in more weeks than I want to count and all you want to do is crunch numbers?"

"Well…" She felt him hardening under her, and her body responded instinctively. Heat boiled low in her belly; her breath turned thick. "That's not *all* I want to crunch."

"Do tell. Or better yet, show."

"I will," she promised. Hiking a leg over his hips, she rolled upright again. "I most definitely will. But I want those numbers."

Travis would have promised her anything at that point. Spreadsheets crammed with EAS test data, diamond ankle bracelets, a cruise to the South Pacific, the yappy toy poodle she'd almost talked herself into some years back. At the time he'd cringed at the possibility one of his crew might spot him walking a white rat with pink bows and toenails on the end of a leash. Now he wouldn't hesitate to parade the critter up and down the flight line if that was what it took to get Kate back.

His mind and body soared. He had her in his arms, in his bed, in his life. He'd keep her there, whatever it took. And damned if this wasn't the perfect start. She looked like a sea siren with her still-damp hair in wild tangles and a seductively wicked smile on her lips as she straddled him. He was determined to take it slow this time. He wanted to watch her skin flush with desire, see her back arch and her head go back as her pleasure mounted.

Only after she'd climaxed in long, tight spasms did he grip her hips and let himself join her.

By the time she surfaced for the second time, a different but almost as compelling hunger gripped Kate. It made itself heard with an insistent rumble from the vicinity of her stomach.

"I need pasta," she moaned. "Lots of pasta!"

"I think that can be arranged."

Recovering far faster than Kate, Travis rolled out of bed with the lithe agility that had landed him a basketball scholarship to UMass.

"We missed our reservation for dinner on the roof, but there's a great little trattoria only a few minutes' walk from here. Not fancy, but really good food."

"I'm in!"

While he grabbed a quick shower, she cleaned up, made a valiant effort with her hair before dressing in khaki slacks and a bright red tank. She'd reached for her purse and was about to sling it over her shoulder when she decided to check her iPhone for messages.

She had a bunch. Scrolling through the long list, she found five from work, one from Cassa di Molino and two from Dawn. The last came with an italicized subject header. *CALL ME!*

Alarmed, Kate hit the re-call button. A dozen gory possibilities blazed through her mind while the phone buzzed. She was a bundle of nerves when Dawn finally answered with a breathless *"Pronto."*

"It's me. I just saw your message. What's wrong?"

"Nothing. Just the opposite, in fact. You should see this villa! It's like something out of *Lifestyles of the Italian Rich and Famous*."

Sagging in relief, Kate dropped onto the rumpled covers as Dawn continued. "It's so over-the-top luxurious, Callie's nervous as hell. She thinks we'll be presented with a bill when we leave that we won't be able to pay and we'll end up in debtors' prison."

"Debtors' prison went out in the late 1800s," Kate countered, but she understood Callie's worry given the fact that her friend was currently unemployed.

"How the heck can an Italian Air Force major afford a place like this?" Dawn wanted to know.

"According to Travis, *maggiore* is only one of Carlo's titles. He's also a prince."

"Prince? Like in royalty or rock star?"

"Royalty."

"Holy crap! Just like in the *Three Coins in the Fountain* movie. Is he as yummy as Louis Jourdan?"

"I didn't ask Travis for a physical description."

"What's his full name? I'll look him up on the internet."

Kate searched her mind. "I'm coming up blank on the last name, but I think he's prince of Lombard and…" She scrunched her forehead. "And someplace else."

"Hold on! I have to tell Callie this!"

Kate waited while Dawn related the news that their absent landlord was a real, live prince. Then Callie took the phone to discuss a far more important issue.

"How's it going with you and Travis?"

"Good." A pause, a sigh and a sappy smile. "Better than good."

"Want to share some details?"

"I will. Tomorrow, I promise."

"You sound happy, Kate."

The soft observation brought tears to her eyes. She blinked them away but couldn't deny the joy behind them.

"I am. And I've got so much to tell you and Dawn. But we're just getting ready to go out and grab something to eat. I'll call you tomorrow."

"You'd better! Ciao for now."

"Ciao."

Travis was waiting when she hurried out of the bedroom. Slinging her purse strap over her shoulder, she issued a hurried apology. "Sorry. I had to return an urgent call from Dawn."

"Is she okay?"

"She is. Mostly she just wanted to rhapsodize about Carlo's villa. She was also as surprised as I was to hear you're hobnobbing with royalty."

He answered with a shrug and the highest accolade he could bestow on a comrade in arms. "Prince or not, he's solid. You ready?"

When they stepped out into night, she discovered that Venice in the moonlight was even more magical than in the bright light of day. The shimmering waters of the Grand Canal reflected a fat, glowing moon and the floodlit facades of its grand palazzi. The tall, narrow dwellings along the smaller side canals lost their slightly decrepit air of peeling plaster and displayed instead neck-laces of brightly lit windows.

With the ease of long habit, Travis slipped an arm around Kate's waist and kept her close as they wove through tourists and locals out to enjoy a late dinner. Two turns, several twisting streets and three bridges later, they reached a tiny square bordered on three sides by resi-dences, several of which featured business establishments on the ground floor.

The Trattoria di Pesce was one of these establish-ments. A string of lightbulbs cast halos over its half dozen outdoor tables. Large plate-glass windows showed an in-terior with rows of wooden booths dominated by shelves displaying red, black and green pasta in glass jars of every conceivable size and shape. At the very rear was a cutaway providing a glimpse of a kitchen with long strands of noodles hanging from wooden poles.

"Trust me," Travis said as they made for the trattor-ia. "This place serves the best crab tagliatelle in town."

"I'll take your word for... Oh!" Kate stopped dead. "Listen!"

Head cocked, she drank in the deep, rich notes of a cello. Spinning on one heel, she followed the dark, sen-suous notes to the church that formed the fourth side of the square. Its doors stood open, spilling light and the cello's deep tones. Moments later, other strings added their voices. A violin, a viola, another violin, then the cello again.

"I think that's a Rossini sonata," she murmured in delight.

"If you say so." Eyes narrowed in the dim light, Travis squinted at a poster in a glass case beside the church's open doors. "If I'm translating this right, it says students from Venice's classical conservatory are performing here tonight." He paused, gave the poster another squint and squared his shoulders. "The concert is free to the public. Do you want to slip inside and listen?"

If Kate wasn't already falling in love with her husband all over again, the heroic offer would push her over the edge. She and Travis shared so many passions. Walks in the pristine stillness of a fresh snowfall. Butter dripping from their chins while they pigged out on steamed lobster. The noise and mayhem when the Boston Bruins took to the ice. A mutual dedication to their work.

Classical music, however, was *not* one of their shared interests. In all their years together, Kate had dragged her reluctant fiancé and then husband to a total of three symphony concerts. After the first, he'd lied like hell in an unsuccessful attempt to convince her he'd enjoyed the experience. After the second, he'd admitted he wasn't quite there yet. Halfway through the third, his chin dropped to his chest and his snores took on the booming resonance of a tympanic roll. Kate had been forced to elbow him in the ribs throughout the rest of the concert to keep other members of the audience from zinging exasperated looks his way.

After that disaster, they'd worked out a comfortable compromise for their tastes in music. She would screw in her earbuds, he would plug his in and they'd hum along to different beats. Live performances were limited to entertainers they both liked. So the thought that he would brave yet another round of bruised ribs to attend a performance of chamber music made her heart sing along with the four-stringed instruments.

"Why not enjoy the best of both worlds?" she suggested, gesturing to the trattoria. "If we sit outside, we can listen *and* eat."

"Okay by me. But," he added as they recrossed the tiny square, "don't think I don't recognize the ulterior motive here. You're hoping a plate of crab pasta will keep me awake."

"Not hoping," she countered. "Praying!"

She needn't have worried. They lucked out and got one of the outside tables. Just enough of the sonata floated across the square to enchant Kate and form easily ignorable background noise for Travis. They ordered a liter of the house *vino bianco* and sipped the light, fruity white while they studied the menu. It was simple, handwritten and all in Italian. Travis did his best to translate the four items offered.

"Those are tagliatelle," he said, nodding to the broad flat noodles draped over wooden dowels at the rear of the restaurant. "Homemade and the specialty of the house. They're served with various seafoods and sauces."

The gray-haired, stoop-shouldered server who'd delivered their wine filled in the gaps. Employing limited English and swooping hand gestures, he expanded on the menu. Travis went with spider-crab tagliatelle in a cream sauce. Kate opted for the porcini-mushrooms-and-scallops marinara. Their dinners came with cucumber salads and a basket of crusty bread perfect for sopping up olive oil and balsamic vinegar.

The string quartet's performance ended halfway through the meal, which Travis wouldn't have noticed if not for the burst of applause and subsequent emptying of the church.

"That was nice," he commented in a magnanimous concession to a music form that still made him all squinty eyed and sleepy.

"Very nice," Kate agreed solemnly.

They lingered over a shared tiramisu before strolling back through the serpentine streets. Most of the gondolas had been docked and shrouded for the night, but a few water taxis still navigated the Grand Canal. The wooden boats moved slowly, their engines throttled back in deference to the late hour. Iridescent ripples from their wake lapped at the marble steps and landing sites of the palazzi lining this portion of Venice's main waterway.

Like the other palaces, Palazzo Alleghri's exterior was bathed in the light of the moon and discreetly placed floods. Its white columns seemed to rise directly from the shimmering water of the canal, while its tiers of arched windows shed a calm, welcoming glow.

Kate was feeling anything but calm, however. She'd departed the trattoria encased in a bubble of happiness and epicurean satisfaction. Those emotions quickly took a backseat to the pure joy of knowing she would sleep in the same bed as her husband tonight. But with each step closer to their hotel, her joy took on a sharp, shivery edge of anticipation that had everything to do with the bed and nothing to do with sleep.

Three times in one night wasn't their record, but it was enough to make Kate purr when she finally snuggled against Travis's side. Mere moments later, she was dead to the world.

Travis lay beside her, breathing in the scent of their lovemaking, feeling the gentle rise and fall of the breast pressed against his ribs. When he was sure she was out for the count, he glanced at the illuminated dial of the watch he'd left on the nightstand. It was just past midnight here, a little past 6:00 p.m. at his home base back in Florida. If his boss wasn't flying or attending yet another high-level conference on the employment of special ops assets, he might still be at his desk.

Moving carefully, Travis slid his arm from under Kate's head and eased out of bed. Although he'd acted blasé about telling the old man that he'd decided to leave the air force, the prospect sat like a dead weight in his gut. Best to get it done and over with.

Since this wasn't the kind of call he could make naked, he pulled on his jeans and took his cell phone into the other room. He almost hoped Hamilton's exec would say he was gone for a day or in DC or even down with the flu. No such luck.

The colonel was in his office, at his desk and in a blistering mood. "I hope to hell you're calling to tell me you're about to wrap up that project at Aviano."

"Not exactly."

"Well, get it in gear. I need you here, dammit."

Travis had faced armed hostiles with steadier nerves than he felt at this moment. Unconsciously, he squared his shoulders. "I wanted to tell you I'm putting in a request to separate from active duty."

"The hell you say!"

"I've received a job offer, a good one, and I'm going to accept it."

The silence that followed was long, stark and brutal. Hamilton finally broke it with a terse question.

"Will this job get you and Kate back together?"

Travis wasn't surprised Hamilton knew about the split. Crews talked; secrets leaked; rumors spread. More to the point, the colonel's wife kept a finger on the pulse of every family in his command.

"I'm hoping so, sir."

There was no silence this time, no hesitation. The

response came fast and straight from the gut of a man who thought his wife was womanhood incarnate.

"Then do it. I sure as hell would."

Travis breathed easy for the first time since picking up the phone. He could feel the relief—and guilt—rolling off him in waves when the colonel barked a final order before cutting the connection.

"Just make sure you haul your ass back here before you separate, Westbrook. You've got a few things to wrap up at this end, too."

Chapter Six

Kate woke to a day that seemed tinted gold around the edges. The bedroom's heavy drapes shut out most of the light, but a few thin rays sneaked through. Enough to brighten the gilt trim on the chandelier and the gold-leaf vines twining up the bed's four flat-topped posts. Stretching sinuously, she was admiring the intricate woodwork when her husband strolled in.

He'd already showered, shaved and dressed. He'd also obviously ordered from room service. She eyed the silver tray he was carrying avidly.

"Please tell me that's coffee."

"Coffee and *pagnottini.*"

"Which is?"

"Sort of a sweet roll stuffed with raisins."

Wiggling upright, she tucked the sheet under her armpits and scooted over to make room for the tray while he tore off a bite for her to sample. It was sweet and yeasty and good. *Really* good!

"Carlo got Brian and me hooked on these little suckers," Travis explained as she savored the delicious morsel. "Wasn't hard to do, since he has them delivered fresh each morning. I'm guessing they come from the same bakery that supplies this hotel."

"Carlo certainly lives the good life," Kate commented. "When do I get to meet this new friend of yours?"

"Well, I thought we could spend today sightseeing in Venice and drive up to the base tomorrow."

Where he would put in an application to separate from the air force. The thought filled her with a pounding eagerness.

"That works for me!"

He tore off another bit of roll and popped it into her mouth. "I called Colonel Hamilton last night, after you fell asleep."

She swallowed the half-chewed lump, felt it stick in her throat. Breathing hard, she got it down before asking hesitantly, "And?"

"I told him I'm putting in my papers."

Her heart thumped painfully. "And?"

"And I'm putting in my papers."

She let that sink in for a few precious seconds. "Did he try to talk you out of it?"

"Actually, he didn't. Just said he'd do the same, given the circumstances."

She should have felt nothing but relief that Travis had taken the first step in what she knew had to be an excruciating process. Stupidly, what she felt was indignant.

"I'm glad he took it so well," she muttered, tearing off another chunk of pastry. "I mean, why should he care if you walk? You've only racked up more combat hours than any other pilot in wing."

"I expect he'll peel a strip off my hide when I get back to base. But until then…"

She didn't mistake either his smile or his meaning. Her indignation on his behalf fading, she finished the thought. "Until then we enjoy ourselves."

"Exactly."

"Just what did you have in mind, flyboy?"

"Well, for starters, I was thinking we could blow off sightseeing and spend the day in bed."

He added incentive by dipping down to drop a kiss on the slope of one breast. Kate gave the proposal the due diligence it deserved before reluctantly shaking her head.

"As tempting as that sounds, I need more than coffee and a sweet roll before we pick up where we left off last night."

She also needed another soak in that decadent clawfoot tub. Travis had stretched muscles last night that hadn't been stretched in too long.

"Let's have breakfast in that rooftop restaurant we didn't get to last night. We can decide where to go from there."

"All right." He conceded the point with feigned reluctance, as if Kate wasn't very well aware he required a man-sized breakfast to jump-start every day. "But you'd better get it in gear. This is the height of tourist season. Lines form early and long."

She snatched another pagni-whatever from the silver basket and balanced it with her coffee as she rolled out of bed. That left no hands for the sheet, which peeled down over her hips. Travis's appreciative wolf whistle followed her into the bathroom.

The realization that it was going to happen, that their lives were really going to take an entirely new direction, filled Kate with as much effervescence as the perfumed bubbles.

She was still high when she made the promised call to Dawn and Callie. Her friends put her on speakerphone, so they both heard the news that Travis was separating from the air force to take a job with Ellis Aeronautical Systems. Their reactions ranged from a disbelieving snort (Dawn) to a careful question (Callie).

"Are you sure that's what you want?"

"Absolutely."

"How about Travis? Is that what he wants?"

"It must be, since he called his boss last night. We're going up to the base at Aviano tomorrow. Travis will put in his papers then."

"What about this big project he's working on?"

Kate hadn't asked him but could reply with absolute confidence. "He'll stay and finish it."

"How long will that take?"

"I have no idea. He can't really..."

"...talk about it," her friends chorused.

Chuckling, Kate redirected the conversation. "How long are you guys planning to wallow in decadent luxury?"

"As long as we can!"

Callie tempered Dawn's emphatic reply. "Another few days. Why?"

"I know Venice wasn't on our original itinerary, but it's too incredible for words. So is the hotel we're staying in. It's owned by one of Carlo's cousins..."

"Carlo, aka the prince?"

"One and the same."

"I've got to meet this guy," Dawn exclaimed.

"Me, too," Kate said. "But back to Venice and the hotel. According to Travis, they gave us a very reasonable rate. I could try to get the same for you if you want to jump a train and zip over for the weekend."

"I doubt Trav would appreciate us barging in," Callie commented.

"Oh, I don't think he would mind *too* much." Her lips curved. "We're making up for lost time. Come if you want to."

"We'll think about it."

The most important contact completed, Kate scrolled through her messages again and made a return call to the bank in Bologna. Signore Gallo's assistant, Maximo, wasn't in, but he'd left a message with his secretary.

"Signore Gallo would very much like to chat with you about changes to the liquidity index."

The secretary's voice and heavy accent sounded familiar, but it took Kate a moment to connect them to the woman she'd surprised in the ladies' room at the bank, fighting tears. The odd encounter stuck in her mind as the secretary extended an invitation.

"Would it be possible for you and your husband to join him for lunch in our executive dining room on Monday? At one o'clock, if that's convenient."

"I think we can work that. If not, I'll call back and let you know."

"Grazie."

She relayed the gist of both calls to Travis as they took the elevator to the hotel's rooftop restaurant for a late breakfast.

"If you don't mind, I'd like to make another stop at the bank in Bologna. Signore Gallo's invited us to lunch. It should work out perfectly with our revised itinerary."

"Which version?" he asked with a grin.

"The one that has us in Venice today, Aviano tomorrow and wherever for the weekend. We could head back to Florence on Monday, with a stop in Bologna on the way."

"Works for me."

"I, uh, also told Callie and Dawn that we would check to see if there were any rooms available here at the hotel in case they wanted to zip over and see Venice this weekend."

To her surprise and secret relief, Travis took the invitation in stride. "Be great if they decide to come."

"You don't mind?"

"No, sweetheart, I don't." The elevator door pinged open, but he held it with one hand and tipped her chin with the other.

"You three have been best pals for as long as I've known you. I'd be happy to squire the Invincibles around Venice during the day." His voice dropped to a husky murmur. "As long as the nights are ours."

Shivers of delight dancing along her nerves, she echoed his earlier agreement. "Works for me."

But just in case, Travis thought as the hostess showed them to a table overlooking the Grand Canal, he might see what Brian had laid on for the weekend. Carlo, too. Never hurt to have a little diversionary tactic available when and if one became necessary.

In the meantime, he intended to sit back and enjoy his wife's delight in Venice, a city he'd come to know and appreciate these past weeks. Not that he'd experienced it in such sumptuous surroundings before.

Carlo kept insisting he owed Travis for covering his ass during a raid to rescue a captured Italian news crew. If so, the playboy prince had more than repaid the debt. Just watching Kate's face as she took in the restaurant's fairy-tale atmosphere tipped the scales in Carlo's favor.

Even Travis had to admit the restaurant would rank

at the top of anyone's most-romantic list. Sunbeams filtered through vine-covered trellises, the buffet was fit for a king—correction, for a Venetian doge—and their table gave them a superb view of the vaporetti and gondolas gliding over the canal directly below.

The extravagant buffet also offered guests a choice of wine, mimosas, Bloody Marys or Bellinis. Although the latter was more of a cocktail than a morning eye-opener, it went with the setting.

"You know the Bellini was invented here," Travis commented as Kate opted for the combination of sparkling wine and peach nectar served in a tall crystal flute.

"I know. At Harry's Bar, where Ernest Hemingway and Sinclair Lewis and a bunch of other literary greats hung out in the 1930s and '40s." When their waiter delivered her drink, she held it up to the light to admire the pale pink hue. "Wonder why it's called a Bellini."

Their server was only too happy to supply the answer. "It is named for one of our greatest painters, signora. When Giuseppe Cipriani, who owns Harry's Bar, combines sweet peach nectar with the wine, he says the color is the same as that of a saint's robe in a famous painting by Giovanni Bellini. So he names his creation in honor of this great artist."

Tucking his tray under his arm, the man beamed with local pride. "If you wish to see this painting, it hangs in the Doge's Palace. You plan to visit the palace, yes?"

"We do. Sometime later today, hopefully."

"It becomes very crowded," he said, echoing Travis's earlier warning. "But the hotel can arrange a tour so you do not have to stand in long lines. Shall I call down to the concierge and see what times may be available?"

"That would be wonderful."

She smiled her thanks but hooked a skeptical brow when the waiter departed. "The lines in Venice can't be any longer than the ones in Rome."

"Guess again. The major tourist sights in Rome are spread out. Here, they're pretty much concentrated around St. Mark's Square and the Rialto Bridge."

Kate acknowledged the point but remained dubious until the hotel's private vaporetto delivered them to St. Mark's Square for a one o'clock VIP tour of the pink-and-white Palazzo Ducale. The Doge's Palace had served as the residence of the supreme ruler of the Venetian republic since the eleventh century.

"Oh my god! I don't believe this crowd."

Grasping Travis's hand, Kate stepped off the boat's gleaming gunwale onto the pier and descended into a teeming sea of humanity. Tourists of every age and nationality jammed the square. The lines that snaked toward the entrance of the cathedral and the palace were epic.

Yet somehow the cheerful throng only added to Venice's nowhere-else-in-the-world ambience. There was no pushing, no shoving, and hundreds of kiosks lined the broad walkway in front of the palazzo. Their colorful offerings ranged from inexpensive carnival masks to gondoliers' straw boaters to lace parasols and every conceivable variation of I Love Venice T-shirts.

Their concierge had worked magic. Either that or the name of the hotel he worked for did the trick. Kate felt guilty bypassing the long lines at the Doge's Palace. Not guilty enough to forfeit their VIP tickets, however.

The palace was as magnificent as the guidebooks advertised. Okay, maybe a little overwhelming. It contained so many opulent rooms filled with so many priceless masterpieces that Kate went into overload two-thirds of the way through the tour. She was as relieved as Travis when they escaped into the bright afternoon sunshine...and thoroughly enchanted when he guided her through the crowd to an outside table at a restaurant in St. Mark's Square.

The restaurant was one of several housed in the elegant arcade that surrounded the square on three sides. Each restaurant featured regimented rows of outdoor tables with different-colored chairs. To Kate's delight, each also offered its own orchestra mounted on a platform under gaily striped awnings. The orchestras took turns entertaining the tourists thronging the square as well as the customers willing to pay astronomical menu prices in exchange for a table.

Kate's residency in Washington, DC, had exposed her to the world of outrageously expensive dinners and drinks. Still, she blinked at prices on the tasseled menu. She was mentally converting the cost of a glass of red wine from euros to dollars for the third time when Travis's cell phone buzzed.

"It's Brian Ellis," he announced after a glance at the digital display. "I left him a message earlier, asking for a return call."

"You're going to tell him you want the VP job?"

"I am."

"Make sure he understands it's contingent on giving me a better understanding of what you'll be doing. I want statistics," she hissed as he hit the answer button. "Risk factors."

"Christ, I thought you were kidding. What? No, not you, Brian." He shot Kate a fulminating glance. "I was talking to my wife. Turns out she wants a little more information about the duties of Ellis Aeronautical's VP for test and evaluation before we sign on the dotted line." He listened for a moment, then nodded. "Sure, we can do that. What time? Okay, we'll be there."

He cut the connection and filled in the blanks.

"Brian says he'll be happy to provide any info you want and suggests we join him for drinks and dinner at his hotel this evening around seven."

"Okay." She tried to gauge his expression and came up short. "Are you torqued that I want more detail about what you'll be doing? I understand you might be. It's just…"

The waiter appeared at that moment to take their orders. While Travis ordered a glass of red and a small pastry for each of them, Kate listened absently to their orchestra's haunting rendition of the theme from *Somewhere in Time* and tried to order her jumbled thoughts.

"It's just that so much of what you do in special ops is classified," she said when they were as alone as they could be sitting elbow to elbow with tourists from a half dozen nations. "When you left on a mission, most of the time you couldn't tell me where you were going or who'd be shooting at you. It's not easy to live with that kind of fear and uncertainty."

"I get that, Kate." Reaching across the small table, he covered her hands with his. "And I wish I could promise you'll never have to live with either again. Problem is, we can mitigate risk but there's no way to completely avoid it. All we can do is counter its impact with as much happiness as we can cram into our lives."

He was right. She knew he was right. But she still wanted some data.

That stubborn determination lasted right up until their vaporetto nosed up to the private dock of Ellis's hotel a little before seven that evening. Like the Palazzo Alleghri, the Gritti Palace had once been home to a nobleman of wealth and elegant taste—His Serene Highness Andrea Gritti, a sixteenth-century doge of Venice, according to the bronze plaque at the canal-side entrance.

The scene that greeted Kate and Travis when they entered the hotel, however, was anything but serene. A small army of black-clad employees had gathered in the lobby. Their expressions reflected deep worry as a team of medics wheeled a gurney out of the elevator. Brian Ellis strode along beside the gurney, looking every bit as grim.

Chapter Seven

"Brian!"

Ellis jerked his head around, spotted the new arrivals and signaled to the medics to wait.

As Travis and Kate rushed across the lobby, he had the awful thought that something might have happened to the executive's young son. When Ellis shifted to greet them, however, he saw the figure on the padded gurney was that of a woman who looked to be in her late forties or early fifties. Thankfully, she had her eyes open and appeared cognizant of her surroundings.

"What happened?"

"Mrs. Wells tripped." Ellis laid a comforting hand on the woman's shoulder. "We're hoping her ankle is just sprained, not broken."

"I can't believe I was so clumsy," the woman said with a grimace. "You can't imagine how many times I've warned Tommy to watch where he was going!"

"We're on our way to the hospital," Ellis related. "I'm sorry I didn't have time to call you and cancel dinner."

"Don't give that a second thought."

"Is there anything we can do to help?" Kate asked, turning a sympathetic smile on the other woman. "I'd be happy to come with you if you'd like some female companionship at the hospital."

"Thank you, dear, but I know Brian will take excellent care of me." She bit her lower lip. "I'm more worried about Tommy. My silly accident scared him."

"He'll be fine," Ellis assured her calmly, then gave Kate and Travis an explanation. "The hotel has sent an assistant manager up to keep him company until we get back."

He exuded an air of cool confidence, but Travis knew he had to be as concerned as his son's nanny. There was no guessing how long they would have to remain at the hospital for X-rays and medical consults. Travis was about to offer their services as a babysitter when Kate beat him to it.

"Why don't we stay with him? I realize he doesn't know us, but if you call up and tell him you work with Travis, we won't be total strangers."

Ellis didn't bother with any polite I-don't-want-to-impose-on-you protests. Relief evident in his blue eyes, he nodded. "Thanks. I'll do that."

Asking the medics to wait one more moment, he strode to the hotel employees gathered by the desk. He spoke a few words to a distinguished-looking gentleman in a black suit and silver-striped tie, then picked up the house phone and asked for his suite.

"This is Brian Ellis," he told whoever answered. "I appreciate you stepping in to look after my son, but I'm sending some friends up to stay with him until I get back. Yes. Yes, that's right. May I speak to Tommy, please?"

Kate had to admire his calm as he waited for his son to take the phone. Ellis was obviously used to dealing with crises, even those that involved people close to him. This glimpse of the man behind the CEO put a slightly different spin on the fact that Travis would be working with him.

"Hey, buddy, it's Dad. No, we're not at the hospital yet. I'll call you when we get there and know what the story is. In the meantime, I've asked some friends to hang with you while I'm gone. Remember me telling you about Major Westbrook? The C-130 pilot who's testing some new avionics for me at Aviano? He and his wife are on their way up to our suite, okay? Good. Mrs. Wells and I might be a while, so you behave. That means *no* more trying to swim in the canal and *no* bombing passersby with water balloons."

Kate's brow rose at the instructions, even higher at the one that followed.

"And no pestering Major Westbrook to take you up for a joyride, bud. I've still got the shakes from the last time you took the stick."

Travis was grinning when Ellis hung up. "He sounds like my kind of kid."

"Yeah, well, we'll see how you feel about that when I get back," the kid's dad drawled. "We're in suite 220. Here's my key card, and thanks again for doing this."

"No problem. Take care of Mrs. Wells and don't worry about anything here. We'll hold the fort."

Kate wished the older woman a speedy recovery and accompanied Travis to the elevator. "Those were interesting instructions Brian issued," she commented. "Think we're up to this task?"

"His kid's only six. I've got twenty-five years and probably close to a hundred and fifty pounds on him. Worst case, I'll pin him to the floor while you hog-tie him with the bedsheets."

Kate laughed, but after hearing some of young Tom's exploits, she couldn't help wondering what kind of mischievous imp they'd be spending the next few hours with.

His temporary babysitter answered their knock and let them into a suite that was larger and even more palatial than their rooms at the Palazzo Alleghri. She could get used to all these gilt-edged antiques and handblown chandeliers, Kate thought as they crossed an intricately inlaid parquet floor to greet their charge.

His hair was a lighter brown than his dad's, and his eyes would have been just as bright a blue if they weren't so worried. When the assistant manager made her exit, the boy's first concern was for his nanny.

"Is Mrs. Wells gonna be okay?"

"We don't know," Travis answered truthfully. "She didn't look like she was doing too bad when we saw her downstairs, but your dad said they'll have to x-ray her ankle."

"She's always telling me to not leave my stuff lying around where someone could trip over it, and I didn't. I didn't!"

His cornflower blue eyes took on a bright sheen as he pointed to a raised dining area. The generous space contained a table with seating for eight and a massive cabinet displaying an array of exquisite Venetian goblets, each one a work of art.

"It was that step," Tommy said, his voice quavering. "We ordered some sp'ghetti for dinner 'cause Dad wasn't gonna be here. Mrs. Wells went to clear my puzzles off the table and missed that step."

Kate picked up on the subtext instantly. "You haven't had dinner? I bet you're starved."

His lip quivered. "Kinda."

"Why don't I check on that order? And if it's okay with you, I'll make it spaghetti for three. We haven't had dinner, either."

The three of them managed to consume an entire loaf of garlic bread, colorful caprese salads, heaping bowls of the Gritti Palace's incomparable spaghetti Bolognese, and—for Travis and Tommy—two servings of gelato.

Obviously still on his best behavior, Brian's son insisted on helping clear the table before he assumed an air of cherubic innocence. "Didya ever play 'Space Zombie'?"

He directed the question to both adults. Travis shook his head, but Kate seemed to recall a spirited match with a young cousin some years ago.

"I think so. It's been a while, though."

The angelic facade cracked, disclosing an expression of Machiavellian delight. "It's on the hotel's kid channel. Mrs. Wells 'n' me started a game, but she gave up at level three. We could pick it up there, if you want."

"Okay."

Shooting Travis a glance that said she knew darn well she was being set up, Kate sat next to her challenger on the luxuriously appointed sofa. Tommy's thumbs worked at warp speed, and mere moments later they were engaged in a life-and-death galactic struggle. When her spaceship exploded for the fifth and final time, Kate groaned and offered Travis her controls.

"Tommy's too good for me. You take him on."

Gleeful shouts and hoots punctuated the next thirty or forty minutes. Kate tucked her legs under her and hid a smile as her husband did battle with his youthful alter ego.

He and Tommy could have been hatched from the same egg. They were both so exultant when they scored. Neither gave an inch, although it didn't take long for Travis to realize he was out of his league. He was going down in flames for the third time when the house phone jangled.

Kate was closest to the phone and took the call. As she listened to Brian Ellis's terse report, her smile slipped. "Oh, no! I'm so sorry to hear that."

Her murmur registered instantly with the two males planted in front of the big-screen TV. One assumed a careful expression. The other's face crumpled.

"Yes," Kate said, her glance zinging to Tommy. "I'll tell him. And no, we don't mind at all."

She hung up and broke the bad news. "It looks like Mrs. Wells really did some damage. Her ankle is broken in several places, and the X-rays show floating bone fragments, so she'll have to have surgery."

"Is she gonna die?" Stark fear erupted in Tommy's eyes. "Like my mom?"

Dear God! Kate shot Travis a swift look. She had no idea what had happened to Brian Ellis's wife. But Kate didn't want to offer her son platitudes and assurances he wouldn't believe.

Travis got the message and moved quickly to put a personal spin on the disaster. "I broke my ankle once, too," he told the frightened boy. "When I was playing basketball in high school. Came down hard the wrong way and felt it pop right there on the court."

"Did you have surg'ry?"

"Sure did. The docs had to realign the bones and put screws in to hold them stable while the breaks healed.

Then I got a cast and had to hobble around on crutches for a month or so afterward."

"But…" Tommy gulped, tears brimming. "But you weren't old, like Mrs. Wells. Old people don't get well fast. She said so herself."

"That's true. Mrs. Wells isn't *that* old, though. Not like, uh…" Travis stumbled for a moment to come up with a character the six-year-old could relate to. "Not like Harry Potter's professor at the Hogwarts academy."

"Professor Dumbledore?" Tommy wasn't convinced but made a reluctant concession. "I guess not."

"Your dad said he wanted to stay with Mrs. Wells until they decided the best way to handle the surgery," Kate told the boy. "So Travis and I will hang with you awhile longer, okay?"

"Okay."

Hoping to distract him, Travis gestured to the TV. "Want to finish our battle? I might be able to come up with a few desperate moves yet."

"No." The reply was small and still shaky, but there was no mistaking the noble sacrifice behind his next remark. "I'd better take my bath."

He paused, and some of his incipient panic gave way to an almost imperceptible craftiness. "Mrs. Wells makes me go to bed at nine. But I can usually watch TV until ten."

"Usually?" Travis echoed, hiding a smile.

"Sometimes."

"Well, this might be one of those times. Let's get you in the tub, champ. Then we'll see if there's anything worth watching on TV."

With the resilience of the young, Tommy perked up instantly. "The kids' channel has lots of movies. I've seen *Frozen* bunches of times but I can watch it again."

* * *

Kate's phone buzzed while Tommy was torpedoing an array of tub toys under Travis's watchful eye.

"We've decided to take you up on your offer to see Venice," Callie told her. "If you think we can get a room at the hotel, we'll jump a train tomorrow morning... unless you've changed your mind."

"Or Travis changed it for her," Dawn groused in the background.

Dawn wasn't going to forgive Travis anytime soon, Kate acknowledged with a smile. Her friends were mighty, and they were fierce. For maybe the thousandth time since third grade, she realized how lucky she was to have them in her life.

"We'd love to have you join us," she began. "But—"

"Ha!" Dawn exclaimed. "Told you so!"

"—we've run into a small crisis here," Kate continued. "Brian Ellis, the man who offered Travis the VP job, brought his young son and the boy's nanny to Italy with him. The nanny tripped a few hours ago and bunged up her ankle. She's at the hospital now and it looks like she'll have to have surgery, so Travis and I volunteered to sit with the boy in the interim. I'm not sure how long our services might be required."

"We can help," Callie said with her usual warmhearted generosity. "We'll take an early train to Venice."

"Do come, but you don't have to do babysitting duty. Travis and I have it covered."

And doing pretty well with it, too, if the high-pitched giggles emanating from the bathroom were any indication. With a sudden, piercing ache, Kate imagined Travis waging bathtub battles with their son. Or hunkering down to have tea with their little girl and her favorite dolls. Or...

"Let me check to see if there's a room available at our hotel," she said, swallowing the lump in her throat. "I'll call you back."

She was poking in her purse for the card with the hotel's number on it when the house phone rang. It was Brian Ellis this time, and he started with a gruff apology.

"I'm so sorry to impose on you and Travis like this."

"We don't mind. Honestly. How's Mrs. Wells?"

"Resting more comfortably now that they've pumped some painkillers into her. Her surgery is scheduled for early tomorrow morning."

Kate could imagine all the strings he'd had to pull to make it happen so quickly.

"She'll be in a cast and on crutches for at least a month," he related, "and may need physical therapy after that. So she's decided to fly home as soon as the docs give her a green light and recuperate with her sister in California."

"When do you think she'll be able to leave Italy?"

"If the surgery goes well tomorrow, she should be okay to travel on Sunday. I've put my private jet on standby." He paused for several beats. "Tommy's mom died during surgery to remove a brain tumor. He was only a baby, too young to remember the specifics. But he's asked about it enough times that he may freak out over all this."

His terse account put the pain Kate had experienced since her break with Travis into sharp perspective. Her husband was right, she thought with a crimp in her heart. There *were* no guarantees. And certainly no ways to completely eliminate risk, whether it came from war, earthquakes or brain tumors.

"Tommy did get a little upset when I told him Mrs. Wells would need surgery," she admitted. "He seems okay now. Travis is supervising his bath at the moment.

Then we thought we might tune in to a movie on the kids' channel, if that's all right?"

"Fine with me. My guess is he'll dragoon you into watching *Frozen*. He's only seen it fifteen or twenty times. Letty—Mrs. Wells—threatened to quit if she had to watch it again."

"I can't speak for Travis, but it'll be the first time for me. So don't worry, okay? Stay with Letty as long as she needs you. We're fine here. And we'll be glad to watch Tommy for you tomorrow," she added, "so you can be at the hospital during the surgery."

"You better check with your husband on that," Ellis said ruefully. "I got the impression he'd planned a romantic interlude with you in Venice. I doubt those plans included riding herd on my lively offspring."

"We're nothing if not flexible," Kate tossed back.

She smiled to herself, thinking how this whole Italian experience had already taken more unexpected turns and twists than she could have imagined.

"And I have reinforcements coming if they're needed. The two friends I'm traveling with called a few minutes ago. They're staying at Carlo's villa in Tuscany but decided to take the train over to Venice for the weekend if I can get them a room at our hotel."

"If not, they could stay there at the Gritti."

Kate glanced around the magnificent suite and didn't even *want* to think how much it must cost a night. "The Gritti might be a little out of their price range."

"No, they would be my guests. Letty's suite is just down the hall from ours," Ellis explained. "Whenever we travel, I always make sure she has her own sanctuary to retreat to in the evenings. She needs one," he said drily, "after a day with Tommy. I'm going to bring whatever she needs to the hospital in the morning. Then

I'll have the hotel staff pack the rest of her things for the flight home. So her suite will be empty. Your friends are welcome to use it this weekend, or longer if they like. It's booked for the duration of our stay."

"That's very generous."

"It's the least I can do after dragooning you into service."

"Let me check with our hotel first. If they don't have anything, we may take you up on that offer."

Or, Kate thought, if the room rate at the Palazzo Alleghri was as exorbitant as she suspected, despite Travis's assurances they were getting a break.

"Whatever works," Ellis said. "I should be back in a couple of hours. I'm just waiting on the surgeon. He's on his way in to discuss tomorrow's procedure with me."

Of course he was. Mere mortals didn't see their surgeons until moments before the anesthetist slapped a mask over their face. Mrs. Wells and her employer obviously occupied a different universe.

"And Kate...?"

"Yes?"

"Thank you. I won't forget this."

"I'm just glad we can help."

She hung up, reflecting yet again on the remarkable acquaintances Travis had made during his stint in Italy. They might not all wear the same uniform, but they sure seemed to have grown as tight as any band of brothers.

A call to the Palazzo Alleghri confirmed that they did indeed have another suite available. And they would be most happy to let Maggiore Westbrook's friends have it at the discounted rate.

"Which is?"

The answer almost stopped her banker's heart. Gulping, she said she would consult with her friends and call back in the next five minutes if they wanted to take the suite.

She hung up with absolutely no intention of calling back. Dawn might be able to swing half of the Palazzo Alleghri's exorbitant rate, but Kate wouldn't even consider allowing Callie to dig deeper into her savings. Instead, she relayed the alternative proposal.

"Have I got a deal for you," she said when Dawn answered.

"Hang on. Let me put you on speaker. Okay, shoot."

"Brian Ellis—the man whose son we're watching— is arranging a private jet to fly the injured nanny back to the States on Sunday."

"A private jet?" Dawn gave a low whistle. "Your hubby seems to be running with a whole different crowd these days."

"No kidding! But back to Ellis. He's taking what the nanny needs to the hospital tomorrow morning and having the rest of her things packed for the flight home. So her suite will be empty, and when I mentioned you guys were coming to Venice, he offered you the use of it as a thank-you to me for watching his son."

"I don't know." That came from Callie. "First this villa, now a hotel suite. I feel as though we're taking advantage of Travis's friends."

"It's your call. But Ellis sounded genuinely sincere." Kate skimmed a glance around the suite. "And trust me, you haven't lived until you've bunked down in an honest-to-goodness doge's palace."

"We'll take it!" Dawn said, overriding Callie's reservations. "I, for one, could get used to living in opulence."

* * *

Kate told Travis about Ellis's generous offer while Tommy fired up the ginormous flat-screen TV in the sitting room.

"Callie was reluctant to accept it," she related, curling up next to her husband on a sofa backed by plump, fringed cushions. "She thinks we're taking advantage of your new pals."

"Well, yeah, we are. But you and I know friendship's a two-way street. You have to give, but you also have to accept each other's gifts graciously."

"True."

Very true, she mused, leaning against the familiar comfort of Travis's shoulder. He toyed idly with a strand of her hair while keeping a close eye on Tommy as he skimmed the movie channels. The boy zipped past the half dozen adult channels, thank goodness, but paused at a shoot-'em-up action drama that promised blood and gore.

"Keep moving," Travis drawled.

As his father had predicted, Tommy opted for a repeat showing of *Frozen*. Halfway through, however, he went out like a light and didn't so much as stir when Travis scooped him up and carried him to bed.

"Whew," Kate murmured when Travis rejoined her on the cushion-strewn sofa. "We managed to make it through the evening with no water balloons or other flying projectiles. Think we'll be as lucky tomorrow?"

"Doubtful." He tucked her against him. "But we don't have to play watchdog tomorrow, Kate. Brian knows how many hoops I had to jump through to get this time with you. He could hire someone to—"

"Yeah, right," she interrupted with a snort. "Like you would bail on a friend in need? Or I would let you?"

YOUR PARTICIPATION IS REQUESTED!

Dear Reader,

Since you are a lover of our books – we would like to get to know you!

Inside you will find a short Reader's Survey. Sharing your answers with us will help our editorial staff understand who you are and what activities you enjoy.

To thank you for your participation, we would like to send you 2 books and 2 gifts – **ABSOLUTELY FREE!**

Enjoy your gifts with our appreciation,

Pam Powers

SEE INSIDE FOR READER'S SURVEY

For Your Reading Pleasure...

We'll send you 2 books and 2 gifts
ABSOLUTELY FREE
just for completing our Reader's Survey!

YOUR READER'S SURVEY
"THANK YOU" FREE GIFTS INCLUDE:
- ▶ 2 FREE books
- ▶ 2 lovely surprise gifts

PLEASE FILL IN THE CIRCLES COMPLETELY TO RESPOND

1) What type of fiction books do you enjoy reading? (Check all that apply)
- ○ Suspense/Thrillers ○ Action/Adventure ○ Modern-day Romances
- ○ Historical Romance ○ Humour ○ Paranormal Romance

2) What attracted you most to the last fiction book you purchased on impulse?
- ○ The Title   ○ The Cover   ○ The Author   ○ The Story

3) What is usually the greatest influencer when you <u>plan</u> to buy a book?
- ○ Advertising   ○ Referral   ○ Book Review

4) How often do you access the internet?
- ○ Daily ○ Weekly ○ Monthly ○ Rarely or never.

5) How many NEW paperback fiction novels have you purchased in the past 3 months?
- ○ 0 - 2   ○ 3 - 6   ○ 7 or more

YES! I have completed the Reader's Survey. Please send me the 2 FREE books and 2 FREE gifts (gifts are worth about $10) for which I qualify. I understand that I am under no obligation to purchase any books, as explained on the back of this card.

235 HDL GJ2K/335 HDL GJ2L

FIRST NAME	LAST NAME

ADDRESS

APT.#	CITY

STATE/PROV.	ZIP/POSTAL CODE

READER SERVICE—Here's how it works:

Accepting your 2 free Harlequin® Special Edition books and 2 free gifts (gifts valued at approximately $10.00) places you under no obligation to buy anything. You may keep the books and gifts and return the shipping statement marked "cancel." If you do not cancel, about a month later we'll send you 6 additional books and bill you just $4.74 each in the U.S. or $5.49 each in Canada. That is a savings of at least 12% off the cover price. It's quite a bargain! Shipping and handling is just 50¢ per book in the U.S. and 75¢ per book in Canada.* You may cancel at any time, but if you choose to continue, every month we'll send you 6 more books, which you may either purchase at the discount price or return to us and cancel your subscription. *Terms and prices subject to change without notice. Prices do not include applicable taxes. Sales tax applicable in N.Y. Canadian residents will be charged applicable taxes. Offer not valid in Quebec. Books received may not be as shown. All orders subject to approval. Credit or debit balances in a customer's account(s) may be offset by any other outstanding balance owed by or to the customer. Please allow 4 to 6 weeks for delivery. Offer available while quantities last.

BUSINESS REPLY MAIL
FIRST-CLASS MAIL   PERMIT NO. 717   BUFFALO, NY

POSTAGE WILL BE PAID BY ADDRESSEE

READER SERVICE
PO BOX 1867
BUFFALO NY 14240-9952

NO POSTAGE
NECESSARY
IF MAILED
IN THE
UNITED STATES

▲ If offer card is missing write to: Reader Service, P.O. Box 1867, Buffalo, NY 14240-1867 or visit www.ReaderService.com ▲

"Ah, Katydid." He shifted her in his arms. "That fierce loyalty is just one of the reasons I love you."

"Care to elaborate on the others?"

"Later," he murmured with a smile that did stupid things to her insides. "After we get back to our hotel."

Chapter Eight

It was after midnight when Brian Ellis called from the lobby to let them know he was on his way up.

"That was considerate of him," Kate commented wryly as she scrambled to straighten various items of clothing that had somehow got all twisted and bunched.

"Like I said," Travis replied with a twinkle in his hazel eyes, "he knows the hoops I had to jump through to get this time with you."

Kate's tugging and twisting stilled. She wanted her husband out of the military, but she didn't want him leaving under a cloud. "You're not missing any critical tests or milestones, are you?"

"Carlo is covering what needs to be covered."

"Travis! Please tell me this leave of absence isn't going to get you in trouble."

"If it does, it's nothing I can't handle."

Kate's heart sank. Great! Just great! As if the fact

that she was forcing her husband to choose between her and the career he loved didn't make her feel guilty enough.

She was still squirming at the thought when Ellis rapped on the door. Travis let him in and offered to return his key card.

"I can get another key at the desk. You'd better keep that one…if you're *sure* you don't mind staying with Tommy the Terrible during Letty's surgery."

"We're sure, and he wasn't terrible at all."

"Ha!" his loving father replied. "Don't let that angelic exterior fool you. He's always on his best behavior with strangers. But in the immortal words of Scarlett O'Hara, tomorrow is another day."

Travis laughed, and Kate picked up on that cue. "Speaking of tomorrow, my friends decided to zip over to Venice for the weekend. If *you're* sure you don't mind them taking temporary occupancy of Letty's suite."

"Lord, no! Now I won't feel so guilty about interrupting your Venetian interlude."

"Did you talk to the surgeon?" Travis wanted to know.

"I did. I also had my people do a thorough scrub of his credentials. From all reports, he's tops in his field."

"What time is the surgery?"

"Ten a.m. I need to get to the hospital by eight," Ellis said apologetically. "I want to be there when they prep Letty."

"No problem," Travis assured him. "How about we show up here at seven?"

"Let's make it seven thirty. I'll arrange for a vaporetto to pick you up, then take me directly to the hospital." He raked a hand through his short brown hair.

"It's been a long day. I could use a drink. How about you two?"

To Kate's relief, Travis took a pass. She was feeling as whipped as Brian Ellis now looked. With his tie loosened and whiskers beginning to bristle his cheeks and chin, the executive was showing the effects of the traumatic evening.

He insisted on sending them back to the Palazzo Alleghri in the Gritti's luxurious private vaporetto. Due to the late hour, the oak-paneled motorboat glided almost silently through the canals. Although light still spilled from a few cafés and trattorias, the residences lining the waterway were shuttered and dark. Gondolas shrouded with canvas bobbed in their moorings, and even the floodlights illuminating Venice's distinctive landmarks had been turned off.

Kate drowsed in Travis's arms for most of the short ride, but when the door to their suite clicked shut behind them, she came wide awake. The strenuous activities that followed wiped her out, however. So much that she groaned and dragged the sheet over her head when the phone beside their bed buzzed a wake-up call at six thirty the next morning.

Afterward, Kate could only blame her lack of sleep for forgetting Brian's prophetic warning. Not until she and Travis arrived at the Gritti Palace did she discover that tomorrow was indeed another day.

"There's still time for you to back out," an obviously exasperated Ellis warned when he opened the door.

"You take care of Mrs. Wells. Kate and I will hold down the home front," Travis assured him with what they both later agreed was totally misplaced confidence.

Ellis threw a dubious glance at the pint-size figure planted on the sofa. His arms were crossed over the snarling dinosaur on his T-shirt and a mutinous expression sat on his face.

"Go," Travis insisted.

Yielding, Ellis hefted the small suitcase sitting next to the door. "I've asked the hotel to pack the rest of Letty's things and move them into our suite," he told Kate. "They'll clean the rooms and have them ready for your friends by noon."

"Great. Last word was they planned to arrive around three this afternoon."

"Okay." He shot his son another glance. "I'll call you as soon as Letty's out of surgery and tell you how it went, bud."

His only reply was a scowl.

With his soft brown hair and angelic blue eyes, the boy looked like an advertisement for Cute Kids Inc. But the real Tommy the Terrible emerged almost before the door clicked shut behind his father.

The first crisis involved breakfast. No, he didn't want to go down to the restaurant. No, he didn't want anything on the room service menu. The oatmeal was too mushy. The cereal didn't contain one single raisin, and they did something funny to their scrambled eggs.

"Okay," Travis answered with commendable patience. "What *do* you want?"

"Nothing."

"Suit yourself. But Kate and I haven't eaten." He threw her a conspiratorial glance. "How do blueberry pancakes and a cheese omelet sound?"

"Wonderful. Order a side of bacon, too. I'm starving. And orange juice," she added with a quick look at the pouting youngster.

"And coffee," Travis muttered. "We're going to need coffee."

Mulishly stubborn, Tommy refused juice and bacon but did force down a half glass of milk, a stack of pancakes and several helpings of thick-sliced Italian toast oozing butter and strawberry jam. While they ate, Kate tried to coax him out of his unhappy mood. He was scared, she knew. No doubt thinking of the mother he could barely remember. She tried to soothe those fears by suggesting a walk to St. Mark's Square to feed the pigeons.

His blue eyes lit up briefly. Too briefly. Then the sullen mask dropped over his face again. "Mrs. Wells says the pigeons are dirty. 'N' they poop on your head."

"Okay. What about jumping a vaporetto and heading over to the Lido? One of my guidebooks said there's a beautiful beach. We could swim and—"

"We have a pool right here at the hotel."

"Well…" Desperate, she powered up her iPhone and searched for kids' activities in Venice. "Have you taken the elevator to the top of the Campanile?"

"What's that?"

"The tower across from the cathedral in St. Mark's Square."

"The big one?"

She didn't trust the expression that flitted across his face. With a distinct frisson of alarm, she nixed that idea.

"This says the lines for the Campanile elevators are a mile long and there's no timed entry. But there are timed tickets for St. Mark's Cathedral. Want me to see if we can get in?"

"Is the cathedral where those big horses are?"

"Yes."

"Mrs. Wells 'n' me saw them when we were out walking, but she said she was too old to climb the steps up to where they are. You could climb them, though. You 'n' Major Westbrook 'n' me."

Kate turned a helpless look on Travis. His shoulders lifted in a you-got-us-into-this-one shrug.

"Let me see if there are three tickets available today."

There were, but only at 2:15 and 5:20. Even with timed entry, the website warned, guests should expect to encounter lines. Kate repeated the warning to the two males at the table. Travis left the decision to Tommy, who made a face but said he guessed he could stand in line…for a little while.

Not reassured by the grudging admission, Kate grabbed the earlier entry slots. To fill the time until then, she suggested they check out the ship models at the Castello's naval museum and have a pizza lunch at a trattoria before heading for the cathedral. Tommy made a show of reluctance but agreed with the proposed itinerary.

When they were ready to leave the hotel, Kate penned a quick note to leave at the desk for Callie and Dawn while Tommy retrieved a ball cap and backpack from his room.

Travis eyed the backpack suspiciously. "You're not toting any balloons or water bottles in that, are you?"

"No, sir." His voice rang with indignation. "Dad said not to drop any more, 'n' I *always* do what he tells me to."

Travis didn't dispute that profoundly questionable statement, but his eyes danced as he ushered Tommy and Kate out into the wild vortex that was Venice at the height of tourist season.

* * *

By the time they returned to the Gritti in midafternoon, Travis was seriously rethinking this whole business of being a parent. He and Kate had always planned to have kids—someday. The topic had come up with less and less frequency in the past few years, but it had still been there, part of his vision for their future. Now he was having second thoughts.

He felt almost as whipped as he had after completing his brutal three-week survival, escape, resistance and evasion training. The SERE course was intended to prepare military members who might be trapped behind enemy lines for the worst. Damned if Tommy the Terrible hadn't tested almost every one of Travis's hard-learned survival skills!

True, the sweltering August heat constituted as much of a problem as the crowds. Kate had kept a viselike grip on one of Tommy's hands, Travis the other. They didn't let the kid off the leash for more than two or three milliseconds, yet he somehow managed to melt into the throng at the ship museum. They found him several heart-stopping moments later with his feet planted wide in the well of a life-size model of a fifteenth-century gondola, pretending to pole his way through rough seas.

At that point a disapproving museum attendant had suggested they depart the premises. Chastened, Tommy behaved himself at lunch, although he put away more pizza than Travis would have believed possible for someone his size. Unfortunately, Brian called while they were at the pizzeria to relay the news that Mrs. Wells's surgery was taking longer than expected. Matters went south from that point.

In quick sequence, Tommy let them know that he was *not* happy about having to stand in line for gelato, the men's room, or to retrieve their tickets to St. Mark's Cathedral. Travis responded with dwindling patience to each of those sullen complaints. The terrifying minutes on the balcony of St. Mark's, however, took at least a year off his life.

It started when they claimed their tickets and a brochure that contained a brief history of the four iconic bronze horses mounted on the balcony directly above the cathedral's main entrance. Tommy seemed interested when Travis related the historical background. That the sculptures were probably Greek in origin. That they'd once adorned the hippodrome in Constantinople and were looted by Venetian forces when they sacked the city during the Fourth Crusade.

His mistake, Travis realized too late, was relating the interesting fact that the Venetians had severed the horses' heads to transport the massive war trophies from Constantinople. Once in Venice, they'd soldered the heads back on and fashioned jeweled collars to hide the seam. Naturally, any kid as lively and inquisitive as Tommy Ellis would want to see the decapitation site for himself. And to do that he would have to hoist himself up on the balcony ledge.

Kate had spotted him first. Screeching, she'd grabbed his dinosaur T-shirt and hauled him off the ledge. When he had both feet planted back on the balcony, Travis did a mental ten count. Then another ten. He was about to go for thirty when Brian called. After relating the welcome news that the surgery had gone well and Tommy's nanny was in recovery, Ellis had asked to speak to his son.

The change in the kid was instant. His face lit up like one of the megawatt flares the Combat King dispensed to deflect oncoming missiles. But despite Tommy's dramatic upsurge in spirits, Travis felt as though he'd been put through a meat grinder by the time they returned to the Gritti.

The message waiting at the desk didn't do much to lighten his mood. Kate gave an excited hoot when she learned that Callie and Dawn had arrived a little over an hour ago. She couldn't wait to schmooze with her pals and bring them up to date on all the happenings since they'd parted company in Rome. Travis couldn't wait to down an early but well-deserved scotch.

Kate's friends rang the bell of the Ellis suite less than fifteen minutes later. Eager to see them, Kate set aside the wine Travis had just poured for her and hurried to the door.

"Look at you," Dawn murmured, searching her face with the keen eyes of long friendship. "You're glowing, dammit." She gave an exaggerated sigh. "If that's what taking a belated honeymoon does for you, maybe I shouldn't have left two grooms standing at the altar."

"Well..."

"Never mind. I'll get it right one of these days."

She breezed in on that rueful admission. Callie gave Kate a fierce hug and followed.

Scotch in hand, Travis rose to greet them. His smile carried that faint tinge of wariness he'd adopted since the two women had declared open season on him. "How was Tuscany?"

"Incredible." Dawn's glance swept the opulent suite. "These new pals of yours certainly live well."

"They do. Can I get you a drink?"

"A red wine would be great."

"You got it. Callie?"

"I'm good for now, thanks."

While he attended to things at the antique cabinet

that housed the bar, Callie greeted the fifth person in the room. He was slumped in a corner of the sofa, regarding the newcomers with a mix of curiosity and shyness.

"Hi. I'm Callie."

"I'm Tommy Ellis."

"Nice to meet you, Tommy. Is that a diplodocus on your shirt?"

His eyes went wide. "You know 'bout dinosaurs?"

"I do. I studied them in school."

"I didn't know girls studied stuff like that."

Callie hid a smile. "Some of us do."

"I've got a book with pictures of tyrannosauruses and pterodactyls 'n' stuff. Wanna see it?"

"Sure."

Perked up by the attention, he bounced off the sofa and showed the way to his room.

"Cute kid," Dawn commented as Travis delivered her a crystal goblet of deep, shimmering brunello. "How's his nanny doing?"

"Last report said she came through the surgery fine and should be able to fly home on Sunday, as planned," he related.

"Kate told us about the private jet." She took a sip of the wine, her green eyes knifing into him over the rim of her goblet. "She also told us this guy Ellis offered you a job. Are you going to take it?"

"That's the plan."

"About damned time you pulled your head out of your ass and got your priorities right, Westbrook."

"Thanks, McGill," Travis drawled. "I was just waiting for your stamp of approval to seal the deal."

Hastily, Kate intervened. "Sheathe the swords, you two. How about we take our drinks out on the terrace? I want to hear more about Tuscany."

After the blistering heat of the day, the terrace was an oasis of shade and soft, sweet fragrance. Planters ringed the stone balustrade, filled with red geraniums that brightened so many Venetian window boxes. At the far end, a lion's head fountain bubbled happily into a marble basin.

None of these feasts for the senses could compete with the color and sheer vitality of the canal, however. Thoroughly delighted, Dawn leaned her elbows on the wide balustrade to admire the water ballet below. She leaned over farther, then had to jerk her hand upright to keep the wine from slopping out of her glass.

"Oops, almost got me a gondolier."

"Better not!" The warning came from Tommy, who'd just come out with Callie. "We're not s'posed to toss anything over the rail. Dad said so. After the hotel manager complained," he added with reluctant honesty.

"Why'd he complain?"

"Water balloons," Travis supplied solemnly.

"Uh-oh."

"It's those stupid hats." The six-year-old's nose scrunched in disgust. "If they're gonna wear straw hats with ribbons 'n' stuff, I think they should 'spect to get water bombed."

Dawn looked much struck by the observation. "You're right. Those hats are stupid. And such easy targets," she added with a glance at the boats gliding by below.

"Christ, don't encourage him."

Dawn responded to Travis's muttered plea by making a face, then moved to the wrought iron beside the fountain. "Sit here with me, Tommy. I want to hear more of your adventures in Venice."

When he settled next to her, the gurgling fountain

drowned out their conversation. The cheerful splash also covered Callie's quiet comment to Kate and Travis.

"He's an extremely bright child. But very concerned about the woman who's been looking after him. I gather she's been with the family for some years."

"Pretty much most of Tommy's life," Kate replied. "Brian said his mother died when he was little more than a baby."

"The father seems to have done a good job with the boy. Tommy's bright and engaging and interacts well with adults."

"He is and he does, although I have to admit he kept us on our toes today."

"I expect he keeps his father on his toes, too," Callie guessed. "Even considering the fact that Ellis can afford to hire live-in help, it's not easy being a single parent. Even tougher when that parent is male. Only 17 percent of single parents in the US are men. As a result, they don't have as many support systems to help them deal with the emotional roller coaster of raising a child on their own."

"Kate and I took a brief ride on that roller coaster this afternoon," Travis related drily. "I haven't looked in the mirror, but I suspect it turned my hair white."

"Pure snow," Callie said, laughing, and gently changed the subject. "Tell me about this new job. Kate says you'll be based out of Washington. What does the job entail, or is that classified?"

"Not completely."

While Travis sketched the bare-bones details of what he would be doing as VP for test operations, Kate thought about Callie's assessment of Tommy. She wasn't surprised her friend had picked up on the boy's worries so quickly. Given her years with the Massachusetts child advocate office, Callie's antennae were finely tuned.

Too finely tuned. The pain and despair she'd had to deal with daily had left their mark on both her heart and her health. She'd lost weight in the past year, Kate thought, her gaze on her friend's prominent cheekbones. So much weight that she and Dawn had begun to worry about the quieter one of their threesome. A primary, if unstated, goal of this trip had been to fatten Callie up on pasta and cannoli.

They'd also wanted to help her forget whatever tragedy had caused her to walk away from her job last month. She never discussed her cases, even with them. Her work was governed by confidentiality laws every bit as strict as those Travis operated under.

Privately, Kate thought part of the problem was that Callie had no one in her life to balance the heartache she'd encountered in her job. Unlike Dawn, who attracted and discarded men with cheerful regularity, Callie approached relationships the way she did everything else, carefully and cautiously. So far none of the men she'd dated—including the half dozen or so Travis had fixed her up with—had made it past her reserved exterior to tap into the passion Kate and Dawn knew she possessed.

She needed someone older, they'd decided. Someone who shared her core values about work and family and friendship. Someone...

Like Brian Ellis.

Almost as soon as the thought hit, Kate dismissed it. The heartache she herself had gone through with Travis these past months had pretty much shattered her naive belief in a perfect match.

They'd complemented each other in almost every

way. Both hardworking, both career oriented, both reasonably intelligent. And so hungry for each other! In those joyously happy first years, neither of them could have even imagined they could cause each other such hurt.

Still… Her glance drifted to Tommy and back again. Be interesting to see if Callie assessed the father as favorably as she had the son.

Chapter Nine

The five of them stayed out on the terrace for another hour. Basking in the attention of the newcomers, Tommy remained on his best behavior. His face lit up, though, when his dad called.

Travis answered the house phone, then passed the instrument to the boy. "Your dad's on his way back to the hotel. He wants to know if you'd like to go to the hospital with him after dinner to visit Mrs. Wells."

Abandoning his manners, Tommy snatched the phone. "Does she want me to come? Really? I miss her, too." His happy glance landed on the geraniums. "I'm gonna pick her some flowers. She likes flowers." He listened a moment, his lips pooching. "But these are pretty red ones. What? O-kaay. I promise."

Heaving a much put-upon sigh, he passed the phone back to Travis. "He wants to talk to you."

Travis took the phone and confirmed that Kate's

friends had arrived and were comfortably settled. "We're all sitting out on your terrace, having drinks and admiring the view."

"I owe you for this," Ellis told him. "But I feel guilty as hell about cutting into your time with Kate. I know you had to hink your flight schedule big-time to get this leave."

"Don't worry about it. Kate and I are glad to help."

"Yeah, well, I may have to hink my schedule, too. I'd planned to stay in Italy through Billy Bob. But with Mrs. Wells out of action, I have to rethink those plans."

Billy Bob was their private code for the final and most critical flight test for the classified modification Ellis Aeronautical Systems had designed for Combat King II. The outcome could mean millions for EAS, possibly billions—Travis wasn't privy to the company's closely held contract negotiations. Not yet, anyway. But he knew EAS's CEO wouldn't have carved this big chunk of time out of his schedule if his company didn't have major bucks riding on the outcome.

"Let's talk about the schedule when you get back to the hotel," he suggested.

He'd kept his reply light. Innocuous. Yet as soon as he disconnected, he found himself the object of three pairs of eyes. Kate's questioning brown, Callie's deep lavender and Dawn's sharp, clear green. Even Tommy had picked up on the subtext.

"Are Dad 'n' me flying home with Mrs. Wells?"

"Maybe."

Emotions washed across the boy's expressive face. Relief, guilt, disappointment...all easily interpreted by the four adults.

"You don't want to go home?" Callie asked.

"Uh-huh, I do. Mostly."

"But?" she probed gently.

"We were s'posed to go to Rome after Venice. I was gonna have my picture taken with a gladiator at the Coliseum. Maybe get a sword 'n' everything."

"Maybe you and your dad should talk about that when you go to see Mrs. Wells after dinner."

"Speaking of which," Dawn put in, "what's the plan? If we're going to eat out, I need to spiffy up."

Kate and Callie shared a quick grin. Even unspiffed, Dawn could bring strong men to their knees. At this particular moment her hair spilled over her shoulders in a careless river of dark red, her I Love Rome T clung to her full breasts and her jeans might have been painted on.

"Why don't we just hit a trattoria for dinner?" Kate suggested. "Travis took me to a fabulous one last night. Very casual."

When Brian Ellis arrived a few moments later, he certainly appeared to agree with Kate's assessment that Dawn didn't need spiffing.

He greeted Callie with a warm smile and countered her thanks for letting them use Mrs. Wells's rooms with the comment that it was small payment for the favor Kate and Travis had done him. But his reaction to Dawn was more visceral and instantly apparent. The handshake was firm, the smile stayed in place, but he did that quick double take Dawn always sparked in the male of the species.

Uh-oh, Kate thought. This could be trouble. As much as she loved her friend, she cringed at the distinct possibility Dawn might wreak her usual love-'em-and-leave-'em havoc on Brian Ellis. The man had lost his wife. He was raising a young son, managing a megacorpora-

tion. Anything other than a light flirtation could prove
a recipe for disaster.

Hard on the heels of that thought came a healthy side
order of guilt. Fiercely, Kate reminded herself that her
loyalty lay—and would *always* lie—with Dawn. Ellis
was an adult. He could take care of himself.

Still, Kate wasn't surprised when he asked about their
plans for dinner, then countered her suggested trattoria
with a generous offer. "Why don't you let Tommy and
me treat you folks to dinner here at the Gritti? Their
indoor restaurant is too formal for us," he said with a
conspiratorial wink in his son's direction, "but we enjoy
eating out on the terrace."

"You'd like it," the boy assured them. "The chef bakes
a special kind of mac 'n' cheese just for me. It's really
good!"

Dawn shot him a quick smile. "Sounds great. I'm in."

The others agreed and they were soon settled at a
table almost within arm's reach of the water traffic gliding by. Spray misters mounted on tall poles dispersed
the last heat of the day and bathed diners in cool comfort. Based on Tommy's enthusiastic recommendation,
they all ordered his special dish. The mac and cheese
turned out to be a truly glorious combination of penne
pasta, crumbled Italian sausage, portobello mush-
rooms, creamy *pomodoro* sauce and four different Italian cheeses baked in individual ramekins.

During the meal Kate surreptitiously assessed Ellis's
interaction with her two friends. After that initial double take, the executive divided his attention between his
guests. He was easy with both Dawn and Callie and
gave only a hint of the issues he was dealing with when
Tommy wanted to know if they were flying home on
Sunday with Mrs. Wells.

"I think so, bud. I'll have to fly right back to Venice, though, so I called Monika Sorenson. You remember the au pair who stayed with us when Mrs. Wells went out to visit her sister in California last year?"

"I remember." The boy's nose wrinkled. "She eats those stinky fish in gucky yellow stuff."

"Marinated smelts," Ellis explained to the others, a smile in his blue eyes. "Monika tried to introduce Tommy to some of her native Scandinavian dishes. Without noticeable success, as you can guess by his reaction. Anyway," he continued, addressing his son, "Monika's fall classes at the University of Virginia don't start for a week. She said she could come stay with you, so I'll fly home with you and Mrs. Wells on Sunday, get you both settled, then—" his glance flicked briefly to Travis "—fly back to finish up at the base. Okay, bud?"

"Okay." Tommy accepted the change of plans with only a grudging poke at the remains of his pasta. "But I really wanted to go to Rome 'n' see the gladiators."

"Next trip," Ellis promised, pushing back his chair. "We'd better head to the hospital and see Mrs. Wells before it gets too late. The rest of you please stay and have dessert. And thanks again for today," he said to Travis and Kate. "Tommy and I really appreciate it. Don't we?"

Recalled to his manners, the boy expressed his thanks with a smile for Kate and a manly handshake with Travis. He was so polite, so well behaved, that Kate might have imagined the sullen, unhappy child of the morning and early afternoon.

Travis had the same thought. He watched the two thread their way through the tables and shook his head. "Hard to believe that's the same kid who got us evicted from the ship museum."

"Then tried to check out the severed horses' heads," Kate recalled with a shudder.

"Evicted?" Dawn echoed. "Severed horses' heads? You're going to expound on those provocative comments, aren't you?"

Kate would have lingered at the table and shared the details of the day's adventures, but Travis had other ideas.

"How about we relate our Tommy adventures tomorrow? I had planned to surprise Kate with an evening gondola ride. When we volunteered for babysitting duty, I figured I'd have to cancel the reservation, but we've still got time to make it." He pushed away from the table. "I'll check with the concierge here at the Gritti to see if they can add two more passengers."

"Sounds like fun," Callie said, rising as well, "but something you and Kate should enjoy together. I'll take a pass."

Her gaze cut across the table and telegraphed an unmistakable message.

"Looks like I will, too," Dawn drawled.

Travis flashed them both a grateful look. Carlo had described the nighttime gondola ride as a small procession of lamp-lit boats accompanied by one containing a singer and several accompanists. It was, according to the *maggiore*, one of the most romantic gifts a man could give his wife during their time in Venice. Outside the bedroom, of course.

And after spending the previous evening and all day today with Tommy, Travis wanted this time with Kate. Only with Kate. An urge she teased him about as they made their way back to the Palazzo Alleghri.

"You didn't try very hard to convince Dawn and Callie to join us."

"Probably because I didn't want them to join us."

"Mmm, I got that impression."

He stopped on one of the little bridges that crossed a side canal. Buildings towered on either side of the bridge, wrapping them in shade, while the competing scents of flowers and dank water tinted the air.

"You know I like—" He stopped, corrected himself. "You know I love your pals."

"Yes," she said softly, "I know."

"But I love you more, Katydid." He buried his hands in her hair and tipped her face to his. "I never realized how much until I came so close to losing you."

This, Kate knew instantly, was a moment she would hold in her heart forever. Travis, with the five o'clock shadow on his cheeks and chin and those white squint lines at the corners of his eyes. Colorful laundry hanging from a clothesline draped window to window on the building behind him. The amused grins on the faces of the two young backpacking tourists who edged past them on the narrow bridge.

"I love you, too." Desperate to imprint every sensory detail, she placed her palms against his chest and felt the strong, steady beat of his heart. "I've spent all these weeks...all these months...trying to figure out how I could live without you."

And years worrying about him when he left on yet another classified mission. Panicking every time she caught the tail end of a news flash about a suicide bomber or attack in Afghanistan or Yemen or Somalia. Feeling her throat go tight when someone on the ultra-private special ops spouses' network she subscribed to became a new widow or widower.

"The stupid thing is," she admitted softly, "there's no real way to prepare for having your heart ripped out.

Except maybe to cram in as much joy and happiness as possible when you can, while you can."

"Seems to me we did a pretty good job of cramming our first three or four years together."

"We did," she agreed, flooded with memories. "Oh, God, we did!"

"That's not to say we can't squeeze in more." Bending, he brushed her mouth with his. "Starting tonight, *cara mia.*"

The moonlight gondola ride more than lived up to their expectations. An astonishingly talented accordion player accompanied the curly-haired tenor. Barrel-chested and exuberant, the would-be Pavarotti filled the air with a soaring mix of operatic and pop classics. Tourists and residents alike stopped to gawk as their small fleet of gondolas glided by.

In Travis's opinion, however, the hours that followed blasted the moonlight sonata out of the water. The moment he and Kate hit their suite, they shoved the aquamarine duvet to the foot of the bed and explored the dips and valleys of each other's bodies as though this was the very first time. They savored every tantalizing taste, every kiss and slow, erotic stroke. As their pleasure mounted, so did their hunger.

Gasping now, Kate arched her back. Travis burned with the need to bury himself inside her but locked his jaw, eased down her sweat-slick body and spread her knees. His palms raised her tight-clenched bottom. His mouth found her hot, wet center. A groan ripping from far back in her throat, Kate rode the waves of pleasure his tongue whipped up.

It was long, languorous moments before she could work up enough energy to return the favor. When she took him in her mouth, his taste was hot and salty and achingly familiar.

Only later, when they both sprawled naked and blissfully satiated, did the thoughts she'd entertained earlier that afternoon drift into her lethargic mind.

"Trav?"

His muffled grunt signified either imminent death by pleasure or slowly returning consciousness. Kate chose to interpret it as the latter. Propping up on an elbow, she stared down at the face bathed in the moonlight slipping through the drapes they hadn't taken the time to close completely.

"Trav, are you awake?"

"No."

"I was thinking…"

Opening his eyes, he regarded her warily. "About?"

"Callie."

"Huh?"

Undeterred by the blank response, she used a forefinger to make little swirls in his chest hair. "And Brian Ellis."

"Callie and Brian?" Travis struggled to make the connection. "Did I miss something tonight?"

"No."

"Then what…?"

"I couldn't help thinking they're perfect for each other." Kate made another twirl in the soft, crinkly chest hair. "Callie's so good with kids. Personally *and* professionally. She's also warm and generous and…"

"And a woman who knows her own mind," Travis reminded her, fully conscious now. "Did you pick up any vibe she was attracted to Brian? Or vice versa?"

"Well…no."

Just the opposite, in fact. The only spark Kate had

registered was that brief flash when Ellis's glance settled on Dawn.

"But think about it," she urged her skeptical husband. "It's like some sort of cosmic alignment. Callie's currently unemployed. She and Tommy connected instantly via dinosaurs. Ellis needs someone to watch his son for the next few weeks and..."

"And he and Callie are both mature, intelligent beings," Travis finished. "They don't need you pushing them into your personal version of a cosmic union."

"I'm not pushing."

"Sure sounds like it to me."

Irritated, she twirled harder than she realized.

"Hey!" His hand clamped over hers. "Easy there, champ."

"Sorry."

She couldn't tell him about her instinctive dismay when Brian had spotted Dawn and done that double take. Or her sharp stab of guilt for thinking her love-'em-and-leave-'em friend might toss Ellis aside with the same carelessness she did the other men who went all stupid over her. Kate owed her loyalty to her friend, not some stranger she'd met for the first time just a few days ago.

She would never, *ever* disparage Dawn to anyone, Brian Ellis included. But there was no reason Kate couldn't drop a few hints about Callie's warmth and compassion and training as a child advocate. Or enlist her husband's help in said campaign.

Being the stubborn, hardheaded male that he was, however, Travis would agree to share his insider's knowledge of Callie Langston only if Ellis asked about her... and if Callie agreed to let Travis act as an intermediary.

"You know she won't agree to that!"

"Yes, I do." Rolling her over, he pinned his wife to rumpled sheets. "Which is why this discussion is moot. And why, Ms. Westbrook, I respectfully decline to take part in any extramarital matchmaking. I've got my hands full managing my own."

Despite his firm intention to steer clear of potential third-party matchups, Travis got sucked in the very next morning.

As usual, he woke before Kate and found a voice mail from Brian on his iPhone, requesting a return call. Tugging on his jeans, he padded barefoot to the sitting room so as not to disturb his still-unconscious wife.

"Yo, Brian. What's up? Mrs. Wells okay?"

"She was when Tommy and I left her last night."

"Still planning to fly home with her tomorrow?"

"Actually, that's why I called you. Turns out she's going to need fairly extensive rehab. Her sister wants her to fly straight to California and stay with her during rehab. Which brings me to the point of this call. How well do you know Kate's friends?"

"Almost as well as I do her." He scrubbed a hand over a bristly jaw as his mind winged back through the years. "I call 'em the Invincibles. They've been tight since the second or third grade. When I married Kate, I knew I was getting a package deal. Why?"

"Tommy and I bumped into the dark-haired one. Callie, isn't it?"

"Right, Callie."

"We ran into her in the lobby when we came back from the hospital. She was heading out to explore Venice on her own. I convinced her that even though this city is safer than most, it still wasn't smart to wander around on her own late at night. Took some effort," he added drily. "The woman comes across as cool and serene, but she's got a stubborn streak on her."

Travis thought of the Callie he'd known for so many years. Quiet. Calm. Indomitable. "I would say she's not so much stubborn as self-sufficient."

"I yield to your better knowledge. Anyway, I talked her into going back upstairs and joining me for a nightcap after I put Tommy to bed."

Well, damned if Kate hadn't pegged the situation after all! Or maybe not. The exasperated edge to Brian's next comment suggested the nightcap didn't go well.

"Callie showed up with the other one. The redhead with the cat's eyes and killer body."

Uh-oh. Travis had heard similar sentiments from other males of his acquaintance. There could be trouble ahead. Big trouble.

"That pretty much describes Dawn," he said carefully, "on the outside."

"What about the inside? Is she steady? Reliable?"

He smothered another curse. Talk about a loaded question. He knew damned well that none of the men Dawn had unceremoniously dumped over the years would consider her either steady *or* reliable. He also knew that he himself still ranked pretty close to the bottom of her favorite-person list after the heartache Kate had gone through these past months.

Yet despite the lethal sniper fire Dawn still aimed his way, Travis respected the hell out of her for her fierce loyalty to his wife. He also respected the formidable intelligence too often overlooked by the men she attracted like flies, most of whom never saw past that killer body…including those two losers she'd been engaged to.

"Dawn McGill and I don't always agree," Travis admitted, "but she's one of two women my wife would trust with her life. And in that regard, I'd say Kate's instincts are 100 percent true."

"Good to know. But should I trust her with my six-year-old son?"

"Come again?"

"It's crazy," Ellis said, sounding even more exasperated. "I still can't figure out exactly how it happened. One minute, Callie's asking about the flight tomorrow and whether I needed any help with Tommy or Mrs. Wells. The next, this fiery-haired sex goddess offers to hang with my son so we don't have to cut short our stay in Italy. What's even crazier is that I'm actually considering the idea."

Just in time, Travis swallowed his instinctive *you gotta be kidding!* Three seconds' consideration produced a more rational response.

"Dawn and Tommy seemed to hit it off pretty well yesterday evening."

"Yeah, I saw that. And I know how much Tom wants to stay in Italy with me. He's a trooper, though. He'll head home with minimal pouting. But if there's a way I can keep him here…"

"Okay, maybe it'll make you feel more comfortable if I tell you Dawn grew up with three older brothers. I roomed with the youngest in college. Aaron used to brag about what a tough little tomboy his baby sister was. Always climbing trees and insisting she could bait her own hook."

"She's still baiting the hook," Brian muttered.

"What?"

"Nothing. What about her work? She's employed, isn't she?"

"She is."

"So how can she put her job on hold to extend her stay in Italy for an additional week or two?"

Travis made another pass at his whiskery chin. "I'm not up on all ins and outs of Dawn's job. All I know is that she does graphic design for some big health-food company in Boston. She's damned good at it, too, according to Kate. My guess is it may be something she can do long-distance."

"Maybe." Ellis blew out an audible breath. "Look, I trust your judgment. Yours and Kate's. I don't take risks where my son is concerned, however, so I've asked my people to run a background check on Ms. McGill. Financials, employment history, criminal record, the works."

"Makes sense. In your position, I'd do the same."

Travis hung up a few moments later, hoping like hell he was in the room when Dawn found out Ellis was rooting around in her private life. No way he wanted to miss that fireworks display!

Chapter Ten

Travis still had a grin plastered across his face when he walked back into the bedroom and found his wife stretching sinuously amid the rumpled sheets. He stood in the doorway for a moment to admire the view.

Her hair spilled across the pillow in a tangle of tawny gold, and the sparse light sneaking through the drapes tinted her skin to pale cream. Then the sheets slid lower, and Travis's blood went south with them. He glanced up from her dark-tipped breasts to find her surveying him with a lazy smile.

"What time is it?"

"A little after eight."

"I suppose I should get up," she said with another languorous stretch. "Unless…?"

The sultry invitation hung on the air. Travis told himself he should grab a quick shower before he climbed back in bed with her. Brush his teeth. Shave off these morning bristles. At the very least, call room service for coffee and the *pagnottini* she'd scarfed down so enthusiastically yesterday.

Coffee and rolls could wait, he decided as he tugged down his zipper. And he'd just have to make sure his whiskers didn't scrape off any of that soft, creamy skin. His good intentions detonated, however, when he stepped out of his jeans.

"Now that," she purred, "is a sight worth waking up for."

The throaty murmur hit with the force of a rocket-propelled grenade. Hunger for her grabbed Travis by the throat and sent him across the room in swift strides. As he yanked the sheet the rest of the way down and rolled his wife into his arms, he realized that what he'd said last night was so friggin' true. He'd never really understood how much he needed this woman in his life until he'd almost lost her.

Despite his best intentions, Travis scraped off several layers of Kate's epidermis before they finally collapsed in a sweaty tangle of arms and legs. She laughed off the irritation on her cheeks, chin and breasts but threatened payback for the angry red patch on her thigh.

He soothed the sore spot with a kiss before flopping onto his back beside her. Only then did his brain unscramble enough to tell her about Brian's call. The news that Dawn had volunteered to supervise Tommy the Terrible for the next week or so snapped Kate's brows into an instant frown.

"I know," he said. "I had to breathe deep when Brian asked if she was steady and reliable."

The frown disappeared. Fire ignited in her brown eyes. Rising onto her elbows like an avenging Valkyrie, she skewered him with a metaphorical sword. "What did you tell him?"

"Whoa! Throttle back, Katydid."

"What did you tell him, Westbrook?"

"That you would trust her and Callie with your life."

"And?"

"And *I* trust your instincts."

Mollified, she dropped back down. Travis could almost hear the wheels clanking as she tried to make sense of this turn of events and couldn't resist yanking her chain.

"Remind me. What was that you said last night? Something about how perfect Callie would be for Ellis?"

She punched him in the upper arm. Hard enough to hurt, dammit.

"Hey!" He rubbed his biceps. "Don't take this out on me. If you don't think it's a good idea, talk to Dawn."

She mulled that over for a moment and shook her head. "I can't."

"Why not?"

"I understand why Dawn bonded with Tommy," she said slowly. "He's a mirror image of her when she was young. Adventurous, inventive and utterly fearless."

"She's still pretty fearless," Travis drawled. "I've got the scars to prove it."

"Okay, but she's also...um..."

"Reckless?"

"Maybe a little impulsive."

"Flighty?"

"Discerning."

"How about commitment-phobic?"

"You'd run scared, too," Kate retorted, "if your parents used you as a pawn in a divorce so vicious it sucked every shred of joy from your soul and ripped your family apart."

"Okay, okay. I get that. What I don't get is whether you think it's a good idea for Dawn to assume nanny duties."

A pregnant silence followed.

"I don't know," she finally admitted. "I like Brian. I'd hate to see him end up as another notch on Dawn's belt. On the other hand, he's a big boy. And he's not walking into the situation blind. He's got us to vouch for her."

"Not just us."

"What do you mean?"

"He's having his people run a background check. Employment history, financial, criminal activities."

"You're kidding!" Kate popped up, her face flushed with indignation. "That's a total invasion of her privacy!"

"Wouldn't you want to run a background check before we left our son in someone's care?"

"No! Okay, yes. But…" She shoved back the covers and snatched up Travis's discarded shirt. "This is Dawn we're talking about!"

"What's the big deal? She hasn't embezzled a couple of million or buried any dead bodies in the backyard lately, has she? Kate?"

She turned away, but not before he caught a glimpse of the guilt that flickered across her face.

"Holy Christ!" Rolling out of bed, he pulled on his jeans and stopped her before she could retreat to the bathroom. "What's she done?"

She shook her head, not quite meeting his eyes.

"For God's sake, you can tell me."

"No, actually, I can't."

"We're talking about a six-year-old here," he said

grimly. "The son of the man I'll be working with. If you're privy to something that could impact Tommy's health or safety, you need to let me or Brian know."

Her chin snapped up. "First, I'm talking about the woman who's been as close as a sister to me for over twenty years. Second, Dawn would never do *anything* that might impact a child's health or safety. Which you should damned well know," she finished fiercely, "considering the fact that she's your friend, too."

She stomped past him, hit the bathroom and shut the door with an emphatic thud. Travis stood where he was, his jaw working. Two minutes ago he'd been sprawled in mindless bliss beside an equally relaxed and happy wife. Now he was staring at a door panel decorated with a painted hunting scene and wondering what the hell Ellis's people might find in Dawn's background that would put Kate in a panic.

This, he decided grimly, called for coffee. And *pagnottini*. A whole basket of *pagnottini*.

Kate emerged from the bathroom, wrapped in one of the hotel's luxurious robes. She'd pinned her hair up and swiped on some lip gloss. She'd also recovered from the shock of learning that Ellis was having Dawn investigated.

His people wouldn't find anything. They couldn't.

Settling beside Travis on the sofa, she accepted a cup of coffee and downed a much-needed infusion of caffeine before tackling the elephant in the room. "I'm sorry I got a little huffy a while ago. And I'm sorry my reaction to that business about a background check worried you. I give you my word—Dawn has done nothing that could adversely impact Tommy in any way, shape or form."

The carefully prepared speech didn't appear to satisfy her husband. Frowning, he studied her with troubled eyes. "We've never kept secrets from each other. Not that I know of, anyway. Makes me wonder what else you won't tell me."

"And that," she retorted, "comes from the man who doesn't tell me 90 percent of what he does every day."

"That's different. It's work."

"How do you know this isn't?"

The reply surprised him. His frown eased, and curiosity took its place. "Okay, now my imagination's engaged."

"Travis…"

"What would a graphic designer at one of the world's largest health-food firms want to hide?" He tapped his chin in theatrical deliberation. "She photoshopped four ounces off one of their models? Artificially corrected the color on a Monster drink ad? Or," he mused, turning more serious, "helped disguise the fact that a vitamin supplement was steroid based?"

"No. No. No. And I refuse to respond to further inquisition."

"Cm'on, Kate. You can't just leave me hanging. Give me a hint."

"No."

To reinforce the point, she popped part of a bun in her mouth. Only after she'd savored its yeasty sweetness for several moments did she reopen communications.

"You were going to take me up to the base yesterday, before we volunteered to watch Tommy. Why don't we go today?"

"We could do that. But this is Saturday. The base will be on skeleton manning."

"I've driven onto a few air force bases," Kate reminded him. "Deserted and otherwise."

"Yeah, you have." The skin at the corners of his eyes crinkled. "Remember the day we arrived at Hurlburt the first time?"

"Like I could forget?"

Kate didn't have to fake a shudder. She'd studied dozens of articles and websites in preparation for their move to the Florida Panhandle. They'd all touted the glorious sunshine, the sugar-sand beaches, the sparkling emerald waters.

For obvious reasons, the glowing chamber of commerce articles neglected to mention the hurricanes that slammed into the Gulf Coast with frightening frequency. Including the one that hit while she and Travis were on the road. It barely reached category two, but its eighty-mile-an-hour winds and angry storm surge had made a believer out of her. That and the fact that the air base had battened down all hatches. Metal storm shutters were rolled down, streets were deserted and runways had been emptied of aircraft, flown out of harm's way.

"Tell you what," Travis said. "I'll see if Carlo's flying today. If he is...and you're real sweet to him...he might introduce you to some of his *men.* They're tough. Really tough."

Which, Kate knew, was pretty much the highest accolade her husband could bestow. Anxious to meet the prince who'd exhibited such generous hospitality to her and her friends, she downed the rest of her sweet roll while attempting to translate her husband's brief phone conversation. She wasn't as familiar with NATO acronyms as she was with USAF terminology, but she was pretty sure *AAOC* stood for Allied Air Operations Center, and NATO 07 was probably the prince's call sign.

"Roger that, Aviano. Thanks." Travis cut the connection and pushed off the sofa. "Carlo should touch down about 1100. I've asked the AAOC to let him know I want to meet with him after his mission debrief. I'll go shower and shave. In the meantime, you could call down to the desk and have a vaporetto ready to pick us up in thirty minutes."

Kate made the call as requested and was about to signal for the operator again and ask to be connected to the Gritti when the phone buzzed under her hand. Startled, she lifted the receiver again.

"Pronto?"

"It's me. Sorry to call so early." Dawn didn't sound particularly apologetic. Then again, she rarely did. "I wanted to tell you I'm making a change in my vacations plans."

"Good change?" Kate asked cautiously. "Or bad?"

"Good. I think. Oh, hell, I don't know. It's all kind of spur-of-the-moment."

"With you, it usually is."

"True," her friend admitted, laughing. "Anyway, I've decided to extend my stay in Italy and stand in for Tommy Ellis's nanny."

"Brian called Travis earlier," Kate told her. "He said you'd made the offer. He didn't mention it was a done deal, though."

"It wasn't, until a few minutes ago. Ellis and I just talked. Evidently he's decided I'm not a psychopath or registered sex offender."

And Kate knew the underlying basis for that decision. She started to tell Dawn about the background investigation. Just as quickly, she changed her mind. Ellis's people had obviously forwarded a positive report or he wouldn't have taken Dawn up on her offer. And she certainly sounded enthused about playing nanny. Why throw a wrench in the works at this point?

"What about Callie?" Kate asked instead. "What's she going to do if we both desert her?"

"I've pretty much convinced her to stay in Venice with me, at least until it's time to fly home next week. I suspect she knows I might need backup with this baby-sitting gig."

"I suspect she does," Kate drawled.

But her mind was racing. Her first thought was that Callie and Brian Ellis might connect. Kate still thought they seemed so right for each other, and nothing Dawn had said yesterday or this morning suggested she harbored any particular interest in Tommy's father.

Her second thought took a completely different direction—the antics of a lively six-year-old would fill Dawn's days. Maybe, just maybe, a sexy Italian prince could fill Callie's.

She'd already Googled Carlo Luigi Francesco di Lorenzo, prince of Lombard and Marino. Although his family's antecedents dated back to the seventh century, their ancient principalities had long since been incorporated into other, more modern states. As a result, Carlo's royal title was now purely ceremonial.

Not that the empty title seemed to matter to the paparazzi. They brushed aside the fact that the di Lorenzos had lost most of their domains down through the centuries and focused instead on their business instincts. The family had invested heavily in various agricultural and industrial enterprises over the years. One tabloid suggested the di Lorenzos now sat on one of the largest fortunes in Europe.

The articles Kate had read about the current prince were no less enthusiastic. They portrayed him as a slightly older but no less adventurous version of Britain's Prince Harry. Not surprising, since both men had opted for military careers despite their vast personal wealth and social obligations, at least until Harry resigned his commission last year. The articles also indicated that Prince Carlo thoroughly enjoyed the company of beautiful women but had stated repeatedly that he was in no hurry to marry and settle down.

The photos accompanying the stories weren't particularly flattering to the playboy prince. He looked short compared to the women he was photographed with. Then again, most of those svelte, impossibly glamorous companions were supermodels and starlets. But Kate thought he also looked a little overweight in his flight suit. When she'd commented on that to Travis, he'd shrugged and said Carlo wouldn't be a major in the Stormo Incursori unless he was fit enough to chew nails and spit rivets.

More curious than ever about her husband's new friend, Kate dressed casually for the drive up to the NATO base in jeans and a coral tank, accented with the colorful scarf she'd purchased in Florence. Travis also wore jeans, and his black cotton crewneck clung to his pecs and abs in ways that turned more than one female head in the lobby.

He hooked on his mirrored sunglasses for the vaporetto ride to the parking garage, where they reclaimed the Ferrari. The VIP parking attendant handed over the keys with obvious reluctance and a last, loving pat on the sports car's fender.

"You want the top up or down?" Travis asked when they'd settled into the body-hugging leather seats.

"Down. Definitely down."

While he engaged the system that folded the top into

its storage compartment, Kate caught her hair back with the scarf. Mere moments later they were on their way.

The route took them north from Venice through rolling hills, small villages and acre after acre of vineyards. The purple smudge of the Dolomites rose in the distance. A branch of the Italian Alps, the mountains grew taller and craggier with each passing kilometer. Kate skimmed the guide to Italy on her iPhone during the drive to familiarize herself with the cultural, historical and gastronomic specialties of the area.

Although it was just midmorning, she had to sample the delicacies. She asked Travis to stop at one of the tasting rooms that lined the road so they could taste different vintages of prosecco—the sparkling white wine made from grapes grown only in that area. Delighted with its bubbly effervescence, Kate recomputed the cost per bottle listed on a slate above the counter from euros to dollars.

"This is as good as any champagne I've had," she commented to the young woman who poured the samples. "Why is it so much cheaper?"

"It is how the wine is processed, signora. French champagne is made the traditional way, yes? It is fermented in bottles, which must be turned and cleared of sediment by hand. This is very time-consuming and...how do you say—with many people?"

"Labor-intensive."

"Just so! For prosecco, the secondary fermentation is done in big tanks. The process requires not so many people."

"Let's buy a few bottles to take back with us," Kate suggested. "Dawn's partial to champagne. She'll love this."

"And she'll probably need it after a day with Tommy the Terrible," Travis drawled.

They decided to drive into the hillside town of Conegliano for an early lunch. The lower, more modern part of the town offered plenty of cafés and restaurants, but a short flight of steps took them to the historic center. Revived by an endive salad and risotto with cuttlefish served in a creamy black sauce, Kate consulted her trusty digital guidebook again and led Travis to see the frescoes covering the exterior and interior of the Scuola dei Battuti.

"'*Battuti* is derived from the Italian word for *beaters*,'" she read aloud. "'It refers to the religious lay order that once occupied the building and was known for its brutal self-flagellation rituals.'"

Travis eyed the frescoes and had no comment.

Once back in the Ferrari, they steered straight toward the Dolomites. Thirty minutes later they reached Aviano Air Base, the sprawling installation in the shadow of the snowcapped mountains. The Italian Air Force ran the base and served as hosts to the Thirty-First Tactical Fighter Wing, the only US fighter wing south of the Alps. It also hosted numerous ground and even naval units from a dozen different NATO countries. With its close proximity to hot spots in North Africa and the Middle East, Kate guessed the crews based at or staging out of Aviano had racked up a sobering number of combat sorties in recent years.

Security was tight, and it took a few moments for Travis to get her signed in at the main entrance to the base. From there they drove through a complex of housing, administrative and support buildings all painted in the military's standard tan and brown. Or in this case, tan and a sort of terra-cotta reminiscent of the tile roofs that capped so many Italian buildings.

When Kate and Travis had reported to their first duty station, she'd commented on the blah colors. He'd explained they were designed to blend in with the terrain. She didn't doubt the monochromatic scheme had served its purpose thirty or even twenty years ago, but suspected today's highly sophisticated satellite imagery probably displayed every structure in ultra-clear three-dimensional detail, right down to the ruffles on the kitchen curtains in family housing.

Drab as the colors were, however, they seemed to welcome her home. So did the signs pointing to the base exchange and billeting office and fitness center. Even the flight line had a familiar feel, with hangars and revetments sheltering aircraft of all shapes and sizes and the tang of aviation fuel permeating the warm August air.

What weren't as familiar were the markings on the various aircraft, at least the ones Kate could spot from the car. She recognized the sleek, lethal-looking US F-16 fighter jets with *AV* on the tail, which designated Aviano as their home base. But there were also small executive jets, jumbo transports, a buzz of helicopters and several odd-looking aircraft she'd never seen before.

"Where's your bird?" she asked, searching the ramp for the squat, four-engine turbo-prop Hercules, the workhorse of US and NATO Special Ops.

"Safely tucked away during the day."

Which meant they only flew after dark, using night-vision goggles. Kate knew her husband was fully qualified on NVGs. He and the crews he flew with had to be, since their missions often involved inserting or extracting a team under cover of darkness at unimproved airstrips deep in hostile territory. The fact that the crews were fully qualified didn't mitigate the danger, though. If anything, the pucker factor increased exponentially with NVGs.

With her husband's life on the line, Kate had made it a point to study the risk associated with the increasing use of NVGs in military aviation. One analysis found that 43 percent of class A accidents due to spatial disorientation occurred during NVG flights. Another concluded that NVG operations increased the risk of spatial disorientation by almost five times.

The fact that this supersecret modification Ellis's company had developed for the special ops 130s involved night flying brought her old fears flooding back. Suddenly, the familiar surroundings of a busy air force base didn't seem nearly as welcoming or comfortable. Nor could she feel quite the same excitement about Travis's prospective new job. Not if it put him back in the cockpit, racking up hours under the same—or even more— dangerous conditions.

She was struggling with that sobering thought when they pulled up to a two-story building. A sign in English, Italian and French indicated it served as the NATO Joint Special Operations Center. Just inside the JSOC was a reception desk. Travis fished in his wallet for a green proximity access badge that contained his photo and several lines of bar code. After scanning it at the desk, he requested a visitor's badge for Kate. Once she'd produced the requested two forms of ID and looked into a camera's unblinking eye, she was issued a temporary pass. Travis clipped it to the neck of her tank top and guided her to a small visitors' lounge.

"Hang loose for a few moments. I'll check to see if Carlo has finished his debrief."

A set of double doors controlled access to the rest of the building. Travis waved his proxi badge a few inches from the scanner mounted beside the doors and disappeared. While he was gone, Kate took advantage of the unisex bathroom to comb her wind-tossed hair and reapply some lip gloss. She was back in the reception area, waiting, when the doors to the controlled area swished open.

Travis reappeared, accompanied by two men in flight suits. One was almost as tall as Travis. The other was shorter, stockier and brimming with energy.

"Ciao, Caterina!"

Carlo di Lorenzo, prince of Lombard and Marino, swept across the reception area. His dark eyes were merry above the black handlebar mustache that bristled from cheek to cheek.

"I cannot tell you how happy I am to finally meet the beautiful wife Travis speaks of so often!"

Chapter Eleven

Kate wasn't exactly up on the protocol for greeting Italian royalty. The prince solved her dilemma by extending his hand as he strode toward her. She offered hers, anticipating a polite shake. Instead he caught it in a warm clasp, bowed at the waist and raised it to his lips. At the last second, though, he angled her wrist so his lips grazed her palm. The kiss was warm, moist and disconcertingly intimate.

Startled, Kate blinked down at the merest hint of a bald spot showing through his curly black hair and almost jerked her hand free. But when he raised his head, the mischief dancing in his dark eyes invited her to share in what he obviously considered a great joke.

"You did not exaggerate," he said over his shoulder to Travis. "She is indeed *bellissima*."

Bellissima or not, Kate gave her hand a deliberate tug. The prince released it with a dramatic sigh. "Why is it always my misfortune to fall instantly in love with other men's wives?"

"Beats the hell out of me," Travis drawled. "Now stop pawing the woman and introduce her to your shadow."

Their bantering wiped out most of Kate's surprise at the prince's too-personal kiss. When she turned to the man who'd accompanied the prince, though, the angry red scar slashing the left side of his face almost threw her off balance again. She couldn't *not* look at it, since it carved a jagged line from his cheek to his chin. But after that first instinctive glance, she locked her eyes on his. Smoky gray and keenly intelligent, they acknowledged her swift recovery as the prince made introductions.

"Caterina, please allow me to present Joe Russo, who refuses to allow me to address him as Giuseppe. He and his men watch my back while I am here at Aviano. Even," he said with another exaggerated sigh, "when I would much prefer they discreetly disappear for a few hours."

"It's a pleasure to meet you, Signora Westbrook."

Like the man he guarded, Russo was zipped into an air force flight suit. Unlike his boss's, however, it molded a lean, muscular frame. Also unlike the prince's, Russo's uniform bore no rank, no flag, no identifying insignia of any kind. Nor did his deep voice give any clue to his nationality. Kate thought she detected a faint accent buried in there somewhere but couldn't pin it down to a country or even a continent.

"You must tell me how your friends enjoyed Tuscany," the prince said, reclaiming her attention.

"Enormously! I can't thank you enough for putting your villa at their disposal."

"I'm sorry they couldn't stay longer. I had thought to fly down to Siena this weekend and perhaps show them the city. From what Travis has told me, they are almost as charming and beautiful as you. And," he added with a sly smile, "I understand that one of them, a redhead, I think he said, can be a very lively companion."

Kate shot her husband a nasty look over the prince's head. Travis held up both hands in a gesture of surrender. "Sorry. Carlo's a master at interrogation techniques."

Of course he was. Special ops had elevated extracting information from reluctant sources into an art form.

"Let me guess," she retorted. "This particular interrogation was conducted after a mission debrief. At a local bar. With several bottles of beer to loosen tongues."

"But no, Caterina." The prince actually managed to appear hurt. "It was at my quarters, with several bottles of wine from my family's vineyard. Which brings me back to your friend. She's in Venice now, isn't she?"

So much for the fantasies Kate had woven earlier this morning about hooking Callie up with the prince. He appeared to be as interested in Dawn sight unseen as Brian Ellis had been at first sight. Burying the thought that both men stood to get burned, Kate answered with a brisk "She is."

"Then perhaps I shall have a drive down to Venice later this afternoon. What do you say, Joe? Are you up for a little R & R?"

"Always. Just give me time to get some men in place and conduct a sweep."

"Of course. Now, Caterina, would you care to meet my crew?"

"If it's okay," she said with a dubious glance at the heavy doors.

"We've finished our debrief. All classified materials are locked securely away."

"Then yes, I'd very much like to meet your crew."

"Bene!" With a gallant gesture, he ushered her to the access point and waved his badge at the scanner.

"Aviano is not our primary operating locale, you understand. Normally we are based at Furbara, outside Rome, which is home to Italy's Special Forces Operations Command. Our detachment here is small, but we are mighty." A smug smile creased his face, burying his upper lip under the thick mustache. "Did Travis tell you the Seventeenth Raiders have logged almost as many combat hours in Afghanistan and Iraq as their British and American counterparts?"

"He neglected that small detail."

"And the mission three months ago? Did he tell you about that?"

"No."

"It was bad," Carlo recounted, his face turning grim as he escorted her down a tiled hallway. "Very bad. A special mission to rescue a news crew taken hostage by Boko Haram."

"I didn't know the US participated in that rescue."

It shouldn't have surprised her. An online article she'd read recently claimed that in 2014 US Special Forces had conducted ops in more than 133 countries— almost 70 percent of the nations in the world. Given the clandestine nature, most Americans had no idea of either their scope or their danger.

Travis replied with a shrug and his usual reticence. "It was a multinational op."

The prince was more expansive. "The African jungle is a bitch... *Scusami!* A bear to operate in. The airstrip we flew into was little more than a hacked-out field, and the rebels were more heavily armed than our intel had indicated. They overran the airfield, and we had to use all our firepower to hold them off so the ground team could scramble aboard with the rescued newsmen." He hooked a thumb over his shoulder at his bodyguard. "Joe earned his pay that day. Your husband, too, Caterina. I would be monkey bait if not for them."

That explained the loan of the Ferrari and the Tuscan villa, Kate thought as they made their way down the hall lined with dramatic black-and-white photos of helicopters and various fixed-wing aircraft in action.

"We learned much on that particular op, Travis and I. That's why we are together again, here at Aviano, to test the modification Brian's company has developed for our aircraft. But enough of such grim matters," the prince said with a dismissive wave. "Prepare to meet my crew, the meanest and ugliest in the sky."

Kate didn't question the "mean" part, but the copilot, combat systems officer and two loadmasters Carlo introduced her to were anything but ugly. One of the loadmasters, in fact, could have modeled for Michelangelo's *David*. His hair was short and curly, his features classically Italian, and his smile could make angels sigh.

As with most NATO crews, they were fluent in English and French as well as their native Italian. They were also not the least bit inhibited when it came to recounting what Kate suspected were highly embellished tales. They couldn't talk classified missions, of course, but their accounts of some of the humanitarian missions they'd participated in left Kate helpless with laughter. The one where they'd rescued an *extremely* unhappy bull from raging floodwaters was her favorite. Then there was the time they'd received the wrong coordinates for an airdrop and sent several members of a ranger squad parachuting through the roof of a bordello. Evidently it was several hours before the rangers finally made it to their designated recovery zone.

The prince played a central role in each hilarious account. And with each tale, Kate's impressions of Carlo di Lorenzo took on new and varying hues. There was the generous friend who'd gone all out to aid Travis in his campaign to reconnect with his wife, the playboy prince depicted in the media, the short, stumpy fireplug who was light-years away from the stereotypical image of a hotshot special ops combat pilot. And now the squadron leader who commanded the bone-deep respect of his men.

Even the enigmatic Joe Russo seemed to hold him in high regard. The bodyguard stood off to one side, arms crossed over his chest and a small smile tugging at his lips as he listened to the ribald accounts.

By now Kate had figured out that Russo's unmarked flight suit slotted him into one of three categories. He could belong to the Italian counterpart of the US Delta Force. They, too, wore no identifying national insignia so—at least according to Travis—the government could deny all knowledge of their existence if one of their highly classified ops went bad.

Or Russo and his team might be civilians, astronomically paid security forces employed by companies like the one formerly known as Blackwater. The prince could be paying Joe's parent company megabucks for a more ruthless level of protection than that provided by conventional forces.

Or Russo and his men could be operating on their own. True mercenaries who hired their guns out to the highest bidder and…

An unexpected arrival interrupted her musings. To the delight of the assembled gathering, Brian Ellis appeared in the doorway.

"I got run out of Dodge," he related with a shamefaced grin. "After I checked on Mrs. Wells this morning and finalized arrangements for her flight home tomorrow, my son announced that he and his new nanny had plans that didn't include me."

"Did they include Callie?" Kate wanted to know.

"No. She said she was going to take in a museum. The Peggy Guggenheim Collection, I think it was."

"An excellent choice," the prince commented. "The Guggenheim Collection is one of the best in the world of works by twentieth-century European and American artists. You must see it while you are in Venice, Caterina."

Kate nodded, her mind pinwheeling with thoughts of Dawn on her own with the lively six-year-old. Resolutely, she put them aside. Despite her friend's occasionally flippant approach to life and love, she was rock solid in every way that counted.

"Actually," Ellis was saying to the prince, "I drove up hoping to catch the debrief from your flight this morning."

"We've just finished, but we would be happy to share the results with you. And with you, Travis, if your charming wife would excuse us for a few moments."

"Sure." She guessed it would take longer than a few moments but didn't want to stand in the way of anything that might get Travis home sooner than he anticipated. "I'll wait in the reception area."

"Or," her husband suggested, "you could take the car and swing by the base exchange in case you need to stock up on shampoo or stuff."

Kate started to reply that the luxury hotels where they'd been staying kept her well supplied with stuff, but she couldn't resist the idea of getting behind the wheel of the Ferrari.

"You don't mind trusting me with your car?" she asked the prince.

His Adam's apple took a quick bob, but he responded with a gallant "Of course not."

She hid a grin at his barely disguised chauvinism and claimed the keys from Travis.

"Just be back by four. Don't forget I need to swing by the force-support squadron."

The quiet reminder put a bump in her pulse. *Force support* was an umbrella term for the unit that provided such varied services as billeting, child development centers, recreational facilities, education programs, the base honor guard and the office that managed military and civilian personnel matters. With a few clicks of a keyboard, an airman or sergeant working in the military personnel branch would submit the request to terminate Travis's military career.

"You sure force support is open on Saturdays?"

Stupid question, Kate realized as soon as it was out of her mouth. With the Thirty-First Fighter Wing flying around-the-clock sorties against ISIS in Syria and other hot spots, its support units would maintain at least a skeleton crew 24/7.

"I called before we left Venice and made an appointment," Travis confirmed. He took a moment, drew a breath and turned to the prince. "Brian knows, so I guess I should tell you, too. I'm putting in a request to separate from active duty as soon as we complete this project."

Shock made Carlo's mouth go slack under his mustache. "But...but you cannot!"

"Yeah, I can. I've already talked to my boss back in the States. It's a done deal."

"So undo it," the prince urged. "You have the best

hands on the stick, the coolest head of any NATO pilot I've flown with. You will make colonel well ahead of your peers. General! Surely you don't want to give up those stars."

"Some things are a whole lot more important than rank."

"Pah! You say that now but…"

"It's done, Carlo."

The finality of the reply cut through the air like a blade. The prince clamped his mouth shut but shot a quick glance at Kate. Although he didn't say anything, she felt the weight of his unspoken disapproval as Brian Ellis stepped into the breach.

"You're looking at EAS's new VP for test operations and evaluations, Carlo. I can't tell you how excited I am to have someone with Travis's experience joining our team. Especially if tests validate the project we're currently working on and the mod goes into full development."

The prince took the less-than-subtle hint and snapped back to business. "We're almost there. Joe, will you escort Signora Westbrook out?"

Signora Westbrook, Kate noted. Not *Caterina*.

After saying goodbye to the members of Carlo's crew, she left with Joe Russo. They retraced their steps down the tiled corridor in silence for a few moments. Then curiosity got the better of her.

"How long have you been with the prince?"

"A little over three months."

"Are you and your men military or civilian or what?"

"What."

The reply was cool and unruffled, but an expression Kate couldn't quite define flitted across his face. Even more curious, she tried another probe.

"So where's home?"

He angled her a glance, his gray eyes as unreadable as smoke. "No place you've ever heard of."

Ooo-kay. She could take a hint when it smacked her in the face. Might as well forget about asking if he was married, had kids, or preferred black-cherry gelato over her personal fave, limoncello and cream.

He escorted her into the reception area and signed her out of the building. Then Kate exited into the bright August afternoon. After the air-conditioned chill inside, the sunshine felt good on her skin. She leaned against the Ferrari's fender to absorb the warmth and the view of the mountains in the distance. Gradually her gaze dropped from the mountains to the hangars spaced at defensive intervals along the runway. She was wondering which of them housed the specially modified transport Travis and the prince were testing when two sleek, single-seat fighter jets taxied out for takeoff.

Once in position, the F-16s waited for clearance from the tower. Moments later their engines revved to a louder pitch. Suddenly the first jet shot down the runway. A second after takeoff, its afterburner kicked in with a thunderous boom and the jet went vertical. The second fighter followed, splitting the air with another thunderclap. Head tilted, eyes shaded against the sun with one hand, Kate watched them soar almost straight up.

The number cruncher in her couldn't help wondering how the latest accident stats for these high-flying, supersonic fighter jets compared to that of her husband's transport. Even with all its offensive and defensive systems, the Combat King too often went in low and slow. Exposed to deadly ground fire, it...

No! She wouldn't go there. Not anymore, dammit! Nor would Travis, thank God.

But the guilt she still hadn't been able to shake nagged at her as she slid into the Ferrari's driver seat and started the engine. She'd met so many other military spouses over the years, men and women who measured their loneliness and worry for their mates against a fierce pride in their service. Kate had felt that same pride. She still did!

Nor did she consider herself a self-centered bitch for wanting her husband to trade his military job for one with fewer absences and opportunities to get shot out of the sky. No, her guilt lay in the fact that she was forcing him to choose between her and a career she knew he loved.

She steered across the base, careful to keep to the twenty-five-mile-per-hour speed limit, as the questions tumbled through her head. Would Travis eventually resent being caught in that vise? Would this decision tarnish the years ahead? Was it worth the risk?

Yes!

That answer came fast and unequivocal. When measured against all the other uncertainties in life, that was one risk Kate could live with.

Feeling better after the stern inner pep talk, she followed the signs for the base exchange. Her military dependent ID gained her entrance into a mall containing a fast-food court, florist, optometrist, dry cleaner and barbershop, as well as the vast, Walmart-like main store. To her delight, the mall also contained a row of colorful kiosks that offered a selection of local products ranging from olive oil and cheeses to Venetian masks and blown-glass jewelry.

One kiosk in particular grabbed her attention. It featured Italian-themed toys and crafts for kids, including an assortment of plastic helmets, swords and shields. Kate shuddered at the thought of Tommy rigged out in the cape and red-plumed helmet of a Roman centurion, swishing a plastic sword in a hotel suite filled with expensive antiques. The fanged leopard helmet and gladiator's trident produced the same reaction.

Hoping a three-dimensional puzzle might engage both his attention and energy, she debated between a model of Rome's Coliseum, Pisa's famous leaning tower and a Venetian gondola. She decided on the leaning tower and had just handed over her Visa card when a trio of uniformed officers strolled toward the kiosk. Two men, one woman, all dressed in ABUs—the splotchy gray-green, slate-blue and brown air force version of battle uniform. It was worn with pant legs tucked into sage-green combat boots and subdued patches and rank insignia on the overblouse.

Kate's idle glance landed first on the man on the left. His rank indicated he was a major, and she was pretty sure the badge above his name tape was that of a communications officer. Then her gaze shifted to the woman walking beside him.

Without warning, everything seemed to fade away. The busy mall, the clatter of boots, the snick of her credit card being swiped. All she could hear, all she could feel, was her pounding heart. She recognized the captain instantly. She should. She'd stared at the picture the woman had posted on her Facebook page so long it was burned into her psyche.

"Sign here, please."

Kate couldn't move. Couldn't breathe. The three officers were only a few feet away now, talking among themselves.

"Ma'am?"

Why hadn't Travis told her Captain Chamberlain

was here, at Aviano? How could he keep something like that…?

"Ma'am? Are you all right?"

The vendor's anxious question snagged the attention of the officers. They slowed, angled toward the kiosk. The major started to say something but quickly realized his companion was the one caught in the crosshairs of Kate's unrelenting stare.

The captain picked up on the same thing. With a questioning look, the slender brunette stepped closer. "Can I help you?"

Kate found her breath and her balance. "No, thanks. You've already done enough."

Confusion blanked the other woman's face. It was perfectly made up, Kate noted dispassionately. Delicately penciled brows, mascaraed lashes, a touch of blush to accent her high cheekbones. A distinctly feminine counterpoint to ABUs and combat boots.

"I'm sorry," she said, frowning. "Do I know you?"

"I'm Kate Westbrook."

The captain's nostrils flared as she drew in a swift breath. Hot color flooding her pink-tinted cheeks, she floundered for a response to that blunt statement.

"I…uh…"

Her embarrassment was so obvious and so complete that Kate actually took pity on her. "It's okay," she said, astonished to discover she really meant it. "Travis told me what happened. He blames himself."

Almost as much as I blamed you!

She kept the thought to herself while the young officer hesitated, still floundering. With a visible effort, she tried to pull herself together.

"Look, I'm sorry if… Well…" She bit her lip, then

threw her two companions a quick look. "I'll catch up with you, okay?"

"Yeah, sure."

They moved off, leaving Kate alone with the kiosk attendant and the woman who'd caused her so much heartache. Standing here, seeing the captain's acute embarrassment, the last shreds of that pain fell away.

"It's okay," Kate said again, more gently this time. "Really. Travis and I have put that incident behind us."

The captain nodded but couldn't quite disguise her thoughts when she asked, "He's here? At Aviano?"

"For a short time. You?"

"My unit's redeploying. We touched down a few hours ago. We'll RON here tonight and fly out in the morning."

She didn't say where they were headed. For security reasons, she probably couldn't.

Kate's reply came straight from her heart. "Stay safe."

Chapter Twelve

Kate drove back across the base feeling like a felon released after a long, ugly incarceration. For reasons she hadn't yet had time to figure out, the encounter with the woman who'd caused her so much anguish seemed to have opened the cell doors. Every shred of anger and lingering resentment she'd had toward Captain Diane Chamberlain was gone. So were the doubts and the guilt Kate had struggled with less than an hour ago.

For the first time in longer than she could remember, excitement about the future bubbled through her veins. She savored the sizzle, the sheer joy of it as she parked the Ferrari outside the JSOC building and waited for Travis with her face turned to the sun.

He exited a few moments later. Although he slipped on his mirrored sunglasses against the bright afternoon sunlight, her first impression was that he looked and moved as if he was as jazzed as she felt.

"Good feedback?" she asked when he approached.

"Excellent! We may wrap this sucker up sooner than anticipated. No, you go ahead and drive," he said when she started to open the car door. "The headquarters building is just a few blocks away." He folded his long frame into the low-slung sports car and hooked his seat belt. "Turn left out of the parking lot."

She followed the instructions, enjoying the muted growl of the thousand or so horses under the Ferrari's hood and the cool breeze lifting the ends of her hair.

"You look happy," Travis commented. "What'd you do, buy out the BX?"

Kate considered telling him that she'd come face-to-face with the captain. Just as quickly, she tossed the idea. The encounter didn't matter. The *captain* didn't matter.

"Not quite, but I did buy a three-dimensional puzzle of the Leaning Tower of Pisa for Tommy. I thought it might engage his attention for a few hours."

Travis snorted. "Thirty minutes, maybe. The kid has the attention span of a flea with ADD."

"Ha! Your mom probably said the same thing about you when you were his age. She's told me the only thing that drained your energy and kept her sane was that you shot hoops for three or four hours a day, *every* day."

Those sweat-soaked hours on the weed-grown asphalt court a few blocks from his home had done more than drain his energy. Kate's mother-in-law was convinced they'd saved Travis from the decaying mill town he'd grown up in. Without them, he wouldn't have won a basketball scholarship to UMass or escaped the gang he'd started to run with.

The scholarship had been his mother's salvation, too. All during high school and college, Travis had worked at least one part-time job. Two when the basketball season didn't curtail his extracurricular activities. After he'd graduated from UMass, reported to pilot training and asked Kate to marry him, she'd begun contributing to the kitty, too. Her mother-in-law was now happily ensconced in a two-bedroom condo in an upscale suburb. She'd made a slew of new friends and, until her son's marriage had stalled out, had been eagerly awaiting her first grandchild.

Which swung Kate's thoughts back to Tommy the Terrible. "How do you think Dawn's managing with Brian's son?"

"My bet is they're doing fine. They *both* have the attention span of a—"

"Watch it!"

"They must be doing okay, or Brian wouldn't have driven up here. And let's not forget Callie's there to help."

Kate wanted to protest that Dawn was perfectly capable of looking after the boy without the assistance of an experienced child advocate. The memory of Tommy climbing onto the ledge of St. Mark's Cathedral killed that thought dead, though.

"Turn here.".

Following Travis's instruction, she took a right and spotted the sign for the Thirty-First Fighter Wing headquarters. The parking lot was almost a quarter full—another indication of the wing's around-the-clock operation, like the two F-16s Kate had watched take off earlier. She pulled into a slot close to the front entrance and killed the engine.

"Do you want me to go in with you?"

"You might as well sit here and enjoy the view. Since

I called ahead, they'll have the paperwork ready. This should only take a few minutes."

"Travis, wait." She reached across the console and snagged his arm. His biceps was smooth and taut to the touch, his skin warmed by the sun. "Please! Tell me what's in your gut right now, this instant. Do you want to do this?"

"Yes."

"Really, truly, honestly?"

"Really, truly, honestly." He leaned closer and grazed her lips with his. "The last ten years have been all about me, Katydid. The next fifty or sixty will be about *us*."

As predicted, he was in and out of the headquarters in less than twenty minutes.

Kate had exited the car and leaned her hips against the hood. Arms folded, she watched anxiously as he emerged and slipped on his sunglasses. She couldn't see his eyes, but the rest of him looked pretty relaxed. And so damned sexy!

Her avid gaze took in the broad shoulders under his black crewneck. The jeans molding his muscled thighs. The sure, confident stride. Excitement percolated through her veins again, and she muttered a distinctly unladylike curse that she had to wait for the hour-long drive back to Venice to get her hands on him.

Or longer. When Travis accepted the keys she held out and settled into the driver's seat, he suggested they host a predinner gathering at their suite at the Palazzo Alleghri.

"Carlo called while I was inside," he said as he put the car in gear. "He wanted to confirm that he's heading down to Venice this evening and is hoping for an introduction to dazzling Dawn."

Dazzling was one of many adjectives Travis used to describe the more volatile of Kate's two friends. She didn't mistake it for a compliment, however.

"What did you tell him?"

"That we'd try to get everyone together at our place around seven."

"Does everyone include Brian and Tommy?"

"Of course. Brian was still at the JSOC, so Carlo said he'd pass the word."

"You don't think that might be a little awkward?"

"Nah. The kid's a handful, but he's basically okay."

Kate hadn't been referring to Tommy. Nor could she articulate why the thought of putting Dawn in the same room with both Brian and the prince made her feel just a little uneasy. It could have been that flicker of pure male interest in Ellis's eyes when he'd first met Dawn, which she'd shown no signs of returning. Or Kate's own somewhat mixed reaction to Carlo after he'd planted that disconcertingly intimate kiss on her palm. Then there was Callie, who seemed to have been left completely out of the equation.

But Travis had already extended the invitation, so Kate dug out her phone. "I'll call Dawn and Callie and see if that works for them."

It did, Dawn confirmed. "Brian called right before you did," she reported breathlessly. "He's going to swing by the hospital on the way back." She paused, sucked air. "He wants to check on Mrs. Wells, so he'll be a little late."

"How's it going with you three? And why are you out of breath?"

"It's going great, and I'm out of breath because I had to scramble out from under the bed to catch the phone."

"Why were you under the bed, or should I even ask?"

"We're playing hide-and-seek. You wouldn't *believe* the places that little stinker can squeeze into."

"Is Callie playing, too?"

"She went back to our suite to… Hey! No fair, Thomas. You can't tag me. I had come out of hiding to answer the phone. No, it is *not* your turn." Another laugh, this one of pure amusement. "You should see the faces this kid can make. Like the one he's showing me now. Oh, Tommy. That's gross! What if your eyelids get stuck like that?"

With hoots of childish glee sounding in the background, Dawn came back on the line. "As I was saying before I was so rudely interrupted, Brian's going to be late. So I'll feed the brat. Then Callie and I will put him in lockstep and escort him to your hotel."

"Okay. See you around seven."

Kate thumbed the off button and sat staring at the phone for a moment.

"Everything all right?" Travis asked.

"Sounds like it. It also sounds as though Dawn might be having more fun than Tommy."

Her husband took the high ground and wisely refrained from commenting. Still bemused by the brief conversation, Kate shoved her phone in her purse and settled in to enjoy the drive back to Venice.

It was almost six by the time a vaporetto deposited them on the landing of Palazzo Alleghri. Wind whipped and sun chapped, Kate detoured on her way to the shower just long enough to consult the room service menu and choose a selection of munchies for their impromptu cocktail party. Fruit, cheese and antipasto for the adults. A fancy—and very expensive!—version of pizza rolls for Tommy.

While she called the order in, Travis iced down the bottles of sparkling prosecco they'd purchased on the drive up to Aviano.

"Better have them bring up some extra glasses," he suggested.

She added the glasses and several varieties of fruit juice for Tommy, then made a dash for the bathroom, shedding her clothes as she went. She wouldn't have time to wash and blow-dry her hair, she decided as she twisted the knobs for the shower's ultramodern cross jets, but she could…

The press of a very warm, very hard body against her exposed bottom produced a reluctant protest. "We don't have time to play, Trav."

"Who said anything about playing?" He pressed closer. "I just figured we could save time by scrubbing each other's backs."

"And while you scrub, I'm supposed to ignore what's poking my rear?"

"Nothing says we can't make this an economy of effort."

She gave a disbelieving snort, but the feel of him ready and eager killed any further protest.

So when Travis nudged her into the spray, she didn't make any noises about the time or the party or the need to keep her hair dry. She just leaned forward and planted her palms against the tiles. And as fast as that, she was ready.

Her belly went tight. Her vaginal muscles tightened. Anticipation combined with the dancing water to send eager thrills racing over every inch of her skin. Suddenly she was too impatient to wait even a few moments while Travis soaped her back.

"'Scuse me." Wiggling her hips, she pushed against his groin. "I thought we were going to economize here."

"So we were."

The hand holding the soap and washcloth snaked around her waist. The other found her center. Blind pleasure shot through Kate as he parted her folds and applied an exquisite pressure. Then he was inside her, lifting her, filling her. She thrust back, grinding her bottom into his belly, squeezing him tight and hard.

Travis spread his legs for better balance on the terrazzo tile while his breath burned hot in his lungs. He was damned if he was going to rush this. He wanted to imprint the sight of water cascading over his wife's shoulders, running down her back, slicking her hips where they joined with his. She wasn't making it easy, though. With every wiggle, every backward thrust, he could feel the pressure building.

Gritting his teeth, he dropped the soap and put his hands on her hips to control the pace. She wasn't having any of that.

"We're not coming in low and slow this time."

She jerked away, and the abrupt separation left Travis feeling pretty much the way he had the first time he'd crashed and burned in the simulator—as if his lungs had flattened and the rest of his insides had gone to rubber.

Thankfully, the hunger stamped on her face told him this ride wasn't over. Blinking the water out of her eyes, she stabbed a finger at the shower's built-in seat.

"Sit!"

The tiled ledge was wide enough to support him comfortably. And low enough for Kate to straddle his hips without resorting to serious contortions.

"This is better," he admitted as she took him inside

her again. Angling his head, he rasped his tongue over a stiff, hard nipple. "Much better!"

He got in only that one lick before she locked her mouth on his and picked up where they'd left off several gallons of water ago. Her hips pumped, her thighs squeezed and Travis gave up all attempts to control her *or* himself.

The shower jets hadn't been off for more than a few moments when the suite's doorbell chimed. Travis was still toweling himself down, but Kate had wrapped herself in one of the hotel's plush robes to attack her wet tangles with her hairbrush.

"I'll get it."

She scurried out of the bedroom and crossed the sitting room, working the brush while hoping to heck that was room service at the door and not one of their guests.

Actually, it was neither. Or at least not one of the guests she'd been expecting. The brush stilled as she smiled a flustered greeting.

"Hi, Joe. Sorry, we're, uh, running a little late." She peered around him at the empty hall. "Carlo's not with you?"

"He's taking care of some business downstairs. I came up to conduct a quick security sweep."

"Huh?"

"Standard procedures." Amused by her goggle-eyed surprise, he held up what looked like an ordinary cell phone with an extended antenna. "Just a check for hidden cameras, scoping out emergency exits, the usual stuff. Mind if I do a walk-through?"

"Oh. No, of course not. Come in."

She trailed after him as he aimed the antenna in a slow arc over the sitting and dining areas. It occurred to Kate that if the suite *did* contain any hidden cameras, someone had sure got an eyeful the past few days.

Travis emerged at that point, fully dressed except for his bare feet, and nodded to Carlo's shadow. "Hey, Joe. The bedroom and bathroom are all yours."

"Thanks."

"Does he do this every place Carlo goes?" Kate asked as Russo disappeared into the other room.

"Pretty much. Kidnappings almost dropped off the scope after Italy passed a law freezing the assets of a victim's family so they can't pay a ransom. But individuals with Carlo's wealth and high profile are still prime targets for blackmail or extortion or even industrial espionage. Joe's just making sure that whatever his boss says or does here doesn't get doctored by some clever film editor and put us all in an awkward situation."

"But...didn't you tell me his cousin owned this hotel?"

"I did, and your point is?"

She was still grappling with the idea of not being able to trust your own cousin when Russo reappeared.

"All clear. I'll get out of your hair."

"Can't you stay and have a drink with us?"

"I'm still on duty."

"The minibar's well stocked with soda and Pellegrino. And there," she said hopefully when the doorbell chimed again, "is room service. If you can't drink, Joe, you can eat. Please join us."

"Well..."

"Good. Now I'll let you two gentlemen handle the setup while I get dressed."

She beat a hasty retreat to the bedroom. The hairbrush got tossed on the vanity. The plush robe joined the discarded towels dotting the bathroom floor. Grabbing a pair of clean, lace-trimmed hipsters, Kate had one foot in when the bedroom door opened again.

Her first thought was her husband. Her second, a curious six-year-old. With a small squeak, she hopped behind the shield of the bathroom wall.

"Travis?"

"Nope," Dawn sang out as she crossed the bedroom. "*C'est moi.* So where did you find that hottie out there in the— Whoa! What happened here?"

She came to a dead stop, taking in the damp towels, the discarded robe, the puddles of water. When her gaze shifted to the woman caught with her hipsters midway up one thigh, her mouth curved in a smirk.

"Never mind. I've got the picture."

Kate shoved her second leg into the panties. "Forget the picture. Hand me that bra and help me do something with my hair."

"Why mess with it?" Dawn dangled the scrap of lace from her upturned palm. "That just-did-my-husband-in-the-shower style looks good on you."

Kate hooked on the bra and snatched up the brush. "Here. Work some magic, and fast."

"I bet that's not what Travis said."

"Dawnnnnnnn."

"Okay, okay. Sit!"

Kate couldn't help herself. "Actually, that's what *I* said."

Eyes dancing, she indicated the shower seat with a jerk of her chin. Dawn followed her lead, saw the abandoned soap and washcloth, and started laughing. Kate held out for all of four or five seconds before she joined in.

They were both still giggling when Callie walked in. "Is this a private party?"

"It was, when the water was running," Kate said, giggling harder.

"And she and Travis got naked."

"And he used the soap to—"

Callie held up a hand. "Stop! I've—"

"Got the picture," Kate and Dawn chorused simultaneously.

Helpless with laughter now, they collapsed. Kate put her back to the smooth tiles and simply slid down until her butt hit the damp floor. Dawn folded her legs and sank with the grace of a ballerina.

Callie shook her head but couldn't hold out against their combined silliness. Drifting down, she joined them. "You two are nuts. You know that, don't you?"

"Is that so?" Dawn poked her in the arm. "So why is Miss Priss 'n' Boots here on the floor with us?"

"Because you look so happy. Especially Kate." A soft smile lit Callie's violet eyes. "It's been a while since you laughed like that."

"I know. I am happy. And oddly enough, I owe at least part of this feeling to the bitch-whore."

Callie and Dawn exchanged startled looks.

"Do you know what she's talking about?"

"Don't have a clue."

They swung back to Kate.

"Okay, girl, talk."

"I met her. Today, up at the base."

Dawn's face went hard. "That son of a bitch Travis! He didn't tell you she was there?"

"He doesn't know. And she's not at Aviano. Her unit's in transit, she couldn't say to where, but they touched down this morning and leave again tomorrow."

"And you believe her?"

"Yes."

Dawn wasn't convinced, but Callie laid a restraining hand on her arm. "Why did meeting the captain make such a difference, Kate?"

"It's hard to explain." She lifted a hand, let it drop. "As brief as the encounter was, it seemed freeing to me. I let go of the anger, the hurt, the guilt I've been dragging around like a damned anchor for so long."

"*You* had nothing to feel guilty about!"

"Oh, Dawn, it wasn't all one-sided. Breakups never are. You know that."

Her friend tipped her chin, and red rushed into her cheeks. Smothering a curse, Kate regretted the reminder of Dawn's near marriages. But before she could apologize, the bedroom door opened and Travis walked in.

He got as far as the foot of the bed before he spotted them in the bathroom, sitting knee to knee on the wet tiles. He stopped short, his brows rising as he surveyed Kate's bra and panties, Dawn's flushed face, and Callie's serene indifference to the wet splotch spreading across her rear, compliments of the towel she'd hunkered down on.

"Is this a private party," he drawled, taking in the scene, "or can the rest of us join you?"

Kate looked at Dawn. Dawn looked at Callie. Their lips trembled. Their eyes brimmed with laughter. It burst from all three of them at the same instant, an uninhibited celebration of friendship and flat-out hilarity.

Chapter Thirteen

The cocktail party was a great success.

As Kate had hoped, the pizza rolls and three-dimensional puzzle totally absorbed Tommy. Not just him, she noted with amusement. Travis's engineering degree and passion for all things mechanical drew him like a moth to the table where Tommy had laid out the puzzle pieces. Travis exercised admirable restraint, however, and confined his input into the construction process to observation and the occasional casual suggestion that a certain piece might fit better somewhere else.

Kate thoroughly enjoyed the tableau they presented—Travis with his dark hair and square jaw leaning over Tommy of the angel-blue eyes and impish grin while the impossibly angled structure rose inch by inch in front of them.

Despite his fascination with the puzzle, Travis didn't neglect his duties as host. He kept everyone supplied with food and drink and contributed to the lively conversation that ranged from Dawn's humiliating defeat at hide-and-seek to Callie's visit to the Guggenheim Museum to Carlo's upcoming participation in a speedboat race in Lake Geneva, Switzerland.

Carlo had claimed a seat on the sofa next to Dawn. Kate and Callie sat across the coffee table from them, while Travis divided his attention between the adults and Tommy. Joe Russo stood a little apart, listening more than participating. If the prince had been surprised to find his bodyguard included in the convivial group, he didn't show it.

Brian Ellis arrived thirty minutes into the gathering with a positive report on Mrs. Wells's condition and assurances for Tommy that he would have a chance to say goodbye before his nanny left for California.

"We'll go to the hospital first thing in the morning," he promised, ruffling his son's hair. "I told her we'd ride in the boat with her to the airport, too. If you're *very* careful and don't try to do wheelies, she may even let you try out her motorized wheelchair."

The boy had been solemn eyed up to the mention of wheelies. Kate could almost see the possibilities whirling through his fertile mind as he showed his dad the construction project. With Tommy busily reengaged, Brian loosened his tie, accepted a glass of prosecco with a grateful smile and joined the two on the oversize sofa.

"Everything go okay this afternoon?" he asked Dawn. "Or do I really want to know?"

"We had fun."

"They took turns hiding from each other," Carlo elaborated, stretching his arm across the back of the sofa. "Dawn was just telling us how long she had to search before she found Tommaso tucked behind a suitcase on the top shelf of your closet."

Casually, so casually, the prince's fingers brushed the curve of Dawn's shoulder. The shoulder nearest Brian, Kate noted.

"The top shelf is one of his favorite hiding places," Tommaso's father admitted with an affectionate glance at his son. "Scared the bejesus out of me the first time I found him there."

"What I want to know is how the heck he got up there," Dawn groused, making a face at the grinning six-year-old. "Your little stinker won't tell me."

"You can't tell her, either, Dad! That's just 'tween us guys."

Brian lifted his glass in a salute to male secrets and asked Callie about her afternoon. She expanded a little on her visit to the Guggenheim, then described taking a good hour to find her way back to the hotel.

Carlo's white teeth gleamed below the black ruff of his mustache. "Getting lost is required of all first-time visitors to Venice. But now that you have fulfilled that basic requirement, there are parts of the city that most tourists never find their way to. Glorious works of art in obscure little churches. Rooftop terraces with views that will steal your breath. Sunsets over the Lido. You must let me show you some of these hidden gems. You and your so charming friend."

His dark eyes glinting, he let his fingers graze over Dawn's shoulder again. The move was more blatant this time and provoked markedly different reactions.

Dawn slanted the prince an amused glance. Callie's response to Carlo's invitation was polite, but cool. Travis looked away and scratched the side of his nose. And when Kate got up to refill the cheese plate, she caught a glimpse of a very cynical expression flitting across Joe's face.

Brian showed the least reaction. Downing another sip of his wine, he engaged Callie in a lively discussion of Venice's lack of a direct route to *any* point on the tourist map. Her natural reserve melted under his gentle teasing, and the animation that came into her face seemed to snag the attention of more than one of the males present.

When Dawn decided to help Kate, though, she recaptured their instant notice by pushing off the sofa with sinuous grace and smoothing her filmy top over her hips. Carlo, Brian and Joe all followed the downward sweep of her palms. Even Tommy looked up, broke into a smile and called her over to check his progress.

Travis, bless him, was too used to Kate's friends to spare Dawn more than a quick glance. He got up, as well, to refill wineglasses, but Brian turned down a refill.

"Thanks, but Tom and I better head back to our place. We have to get to the hospital early tomorrow morning," he added when his son protested. "We're accompanying Mrs. Wells to the airport, remember?"

"Oh, yeah. But my puzzle…"

Travis was ready with a solution. Retrieving the box they'd transported the prosecco in, he tore off one of the lid flaps. "Here. Let's slide this piece under the tower, then place it inside the box. The unassembled pieces can go back in their original carton."

Everyone held their breath during the delicate maneuver, but the half-constructed tower made a safe transition to the wine box. While Tommy and Travis gathered the rest of the pieces, Brian used the house phone to call down to the desk for a water taxi.

With only a little prompting from his dad, the boy

thanked Travis and Kate again for the puzzle and said good-night to Callie, the prince and Joe Russo before beaming a smile at his substitute nanny.

"See ya tomorrow, Dawn."

"See ya, dude."

The Ellises' departure turned the others' thoughts to dinner, and Carlo immediately took charge. "You must allow me to take you to my favorite place to dine in Venice. I'll just make a call, yes, and have them ready a table for us."

Callie tried to bow out, but the prince wouldn't hear of it. "No, you must come. It's an experience you'll not soon forget."

His call made, Joe got on *his* phone and sent one of his men ahead to do a sweep. While that was in progress, Dawn gestured to her snug white ankle slacks and filmy top.

"Do we need to change?"

"But no, *cara*." Carlo's reply was low and warm, his glance a caress. "You are perfect just as you are."

"Careful, Your Highness. Flattery will get you everywhere."

A thoroughly delighted Carlo tucked her arm into his side. "It's hardly flattery when one speaks only the truth. But let's have dinner, shall we, and see where more such truth leads."

The two of them should have looked like everyone's stereotype of a rich man with his latest toy—the tall, voluptuous redhead clinging to the arm of a stocky fireplug of a man some six or eight inches shorter. But Dawn's bubbling personality took the prince's obvious admiration out of the realm of the ridiculous and made it completely understandable.

Still, Kate and Callie shared a quick been-there, done-that glance as they gathered their purses and left.

The next four hours turned out to be a total delight. The prince was obviously smitten with Dawn but included both Kate and Callie in his exaggerated gallantries. And the restaurant he took them to was something out of a dream.

Their vaporetto drew up at the landing of what looked like a private palace. Flaming torches illuminated the elaborate facade. A footman in silks, lace and a powdered wig escorted them up a flight of stairs to a marble-floored foyer lit by hundreds of candles. Joe had them wait there while he conferred with the associate he'd sent ahead. A tall, lanky African-American with a Texas twang, the associate gave the green light.

Carlo didn't press when Joe declined to join them for dinner, leading Kate to think the two men probably preferred not to cross the line between personal and business. Then the footman escorted them into a small private dining room that was right out of fifteenth-century Venice. Candles flickered in tall stands. The table was dark, elaborately carved and set with gold plates. Handblown glass goblets in six different sizes added brilliant, gem-like colors to the table, while delicate notes from a lute and harpsichord drifted from hidden speakers.

Like the footman, the servers who swept in with crystal flagons of wine wore silks and lace and powdered wigs. They presented no menus. Instead, the guests feasted on a meal that proceeded course by stately course. Like the servers and the place settings, each course replicated epicurean masterpieces from the height of the Venetian empire.

It was almost 1:00 a.m. when they finally rolled out of the dining room. Joe must have been alerted by the servers. He met them at the stairs that led down to the landing and assisted them into the vaporetto he had waiting.

As they wound through the moonlit canals, Carlo suggested another stop. "You must let me take you to the Club Blu. The jazz is the best you'll hear this side of the Atlantic."

"Thank you, but I'll pass," Callie said firmly. "After that wonderful dinner and all the hours I walked today, I'm calling it a night."

Carlo made a gallant attempt to change her mind. Ditto Kate's and Travis's, but it was obvious to all concerned that the prince wasn't disappointed to have Dawn to himself.

Callie got off first at the Gritti Palace. Kate and Travis disembarked next at the Palazzo Alleghri. They lingered on the landing, watching as the vaporetto glided away. Dawn and the prince lounged shoulder to shoulder in the rear compartment, Joe standing up front next to the driver.

Travis broke the small silence they left in their wake. "Any bets as to when we'll see Ms. McGill again?"

Kate chose not to place a wager.

To her surprise, Dawn buzzed Kate's cell phone while she and Travis were at breakfast. After the monster meal last night, they'd opted for coffee and a basket of rolls consumed in lazy leisure on their balcony overlooking the Grand Canal.

"You're up early," Kate said by way of greeting.

"Things to do, people to see, places to go," Dawn chirped, sounding bright and cheerful and un-hungover.

"Are you still flying home from Rome with Callie on Wednesday?"

"That's the plan."

And Travis would follow as soon as he wrapped his special project. Until he did, Kate intended to keep *very* busy. They'd already discussed recombining households. Travis didn't care where they lived as long as they were together, so she planned to see if her upscale DC condo complex had a larger unit available. If they did, she would move and get the new place ready for dual occupancy. If not, she'd have to scout out another complex or start looking at homes.

Busy reviewing her mental to-do, it took a second or two for Kate to wonder what had prompted Dawn's question. Several reasons jumped into her mind, including the possibility that her impulsive friend had made some spur-of-the-moment arrangements with the prince.

"Why?" she asked cautiously. "Have you changed your mind about extending your stay in Italy to look after Tommy the Terrible?"

"No. Why would I?"

"Well, you and Carlo seemed to be getting pretty chummy last night."

"We had a great time. He's a sweet little pooh bear, isn't he?"

Kate blinked, but decided not to suggest a major in Italy's elite special ops unit might wince at that characterization.

"If you say so. So what's up?"

"I talked to Brian before he and Tommy left for the hospital this morning. Since you and Callie don't have to check in for your flight until Wednesday afternoon, she's planning to take the early train down to Rome that morning. I thought Tommy and I might go with her. We'd see you two off at the airport, then head into town so the kid can do his gladiator thing at the Coliseum, then zip back up to Venice that evening."

Kate couldn't help remembering the moments of sheer terror she'd experienced when Tommy had climbed up on the ledge at St. Mark's and shuddered to think of the trouble he might get into in Rome.

"Was Brian okay with that?"

"He was, when I told him I would strong-arm Travis into going to the Coliseum with us. I know the Ferrari's only a two-seater, so he'll have to leave it at the airport and train into the city with us. Think he might be up for that?"

"Hang on. I'll let you ask him."

She passed Travis the phone and grinned while he listed at least a dozen different reasons why turning Thomas Ellis loose on Rome was a terrible idea. He eventually caved, though, as Kate knew he would.

"Don't look so put-upon," she said when he disconnected. "Dawn's always had your number. Under that tough, macho exterior she knows you're as soft a touch as her new pooh bear."

Travis's face went blank for a moment, then lit with unholy glee. "That's how she referred to Carlo? Her pooh bear?"

"Her sweet little pooh bear, to be exact."

"Good God! Wait until that works its way back to his crew."

Which it would, Kate guessed, aided by an oh-so-casual comment or two from Travis. She wasn't wrong. Looking positively diabolical at the prospect, he reached for her hand and ejected her from her chair. "We've only got this one day left in Venice. Let's get out and enjoy it."

* * *

They did. So much that the rest of the time flew by and Kate regretted that she and Travis weren't extending their stay in Venice until Wednesday, as Callie and Dawn were.

But she'd agreed to have lunch with Signore Gallo in Bologna. So early the next morning, she slipped into her caramel-colored knit pants. She left the matching jacket off this time. Instead, she paired the pants with a short-sleeved black top and the necklace Travis had insisted on buying during their yesterday's foray to the shops lining the Rialto Bridge. A swirl of turquoise, black and twenty-four-karat gold, the Murano glass heart dangling in the center was as big as a fist and cost more than Kate cared to think about.

Packed and ready to hit the road, she and Travis checked out of the Palazzo Alleghri and took a vaporetto to the car park, where they reclaimed the Ferrari. Travis had timed the drive so they would arrive in Bologna with a comfortable margin before their one o'clock appointment. Since they knew the bank's location and were confident Signore Gallo's efficient assistant would reserve a parking space again, they spent the extra time exploring Bologna's historic center.

They strolled into the bank a few minutes before one. Maximo was waiting for them and once again escorted them up the wide, curving staircase. As before, Kate asked him and Travis to wait a moment while she ducked into the ladies' room to freshen her makeup.

She encountered no sobbing occupant with arms braced on the sides of the sink this time. But she recognized the woman when she and the two men entered the bank president's outer office. The secretary returned Kate's smile with a hesitant one of her own and quickly obeyed Maximo's instruction to advise their boss that his guests had arrived.

The leonine Signore Gallo emerged from his office wreathed in smiles and fervent hopes that Kate and Travis had enjoyed their time in Venice. Mere moments later, the three of them were ensconced in an executive dining room paneled in dark oak and lined with more portraits of the bank's medieval founders.

The consummate host, Signore Gallo engaged Travis in the conversation by keeping it light and nonfiscal through the appetizers and pasta course. The heavy stuff came with the veal *picatta*. Bravely, Travis soldiered through a lengthy discussion of the liquidity index and analysis of the latest stats concerning high-volume bond market issuance.

They lost him over coffee, tiramisu and long-term yields. Although Kate and Signore Gallo were enthusiastic over the fact that low-level volatility appeared to coincide with a rapid growth of cross-border banking, Travis looked as though his eyes might roll back in his head at any moment. Kate took pity on him and was about to thank Signore Gallo for a wonderful lunch when the banker extended an unexpected and completely astounding offer.

"I must confess I'm quite impressed with your work at the World Bank, Signora Westbrook. You've come so far, so fast."

Not hard to do, Kate thought ruefully, when you lost the husband who constituted your entire universe and put your whole heart and soul into your job instead.

"If you will permit me," Gallo continued, "I should like to propose you for membership in the IBA. A vacancy on our junior associates' committee just occurred, and we are anxious to fill it."

Kate's jaw dropped. Literally and figuratively. The blandly labeled International Bankers' Association was, in fact, an exclusive and *extremely* chauvinistic gentlemen's club. Membership was limited to a dozen or so heads of banking consortiums with assets and investments totaling trillions of dollars. The IBA's junior associates' subcommittee was almost as exclusive. As far as Kate knew, no woman had ever been admitted to its ranks. That Signore Gallo would propose her for membership was beyond incredible.

"I'm stunned. I don't know what to say."

He responded with an understanding nod. "It's a great honor for someone as young as you to be put up for membership. And a great responsibility. But everything I read about you reinforces the opinion I've formed in our brief acquaintance. You'll be required to attend quarterly meetings in Bern, of course, but the IBA will cover all travel expenses. So a simple yes is all I need at this point to forward your name to the nominating committee."

Yes! Yes, yes, yes!

Kate was a half breath away from shouting an agreement when her business sense kicked in. How stupid would she be to agree to something this momentous without taking time to weigh the pros and cons?

And chief among those cons, she realized belatedly, would be the required attendance at IBA's quarterly meetings. Including travel time, she could expect to spend days, if not weeks, in Switzerland every three months.

Travis must have weighed the same pros and cons. His grin had stretched wide and proud when Signore Gallo first extended the invitation. It had pretty much disappeared now.

"I can't tell you how honored I am," Kate responded. "May I think about this and get back to you?"

Signore Gallo stared at her with undisguised astonishment. Not surprising, since she was probably the first woman to be invited into the centuries-old, all-male enclave.

"Of course," he said after an uncomfortable moment. "The vacancy will be filled quickly, however. Please let me know your decision as soon as possible."

"I will," she promised.

Once again Maximo appeared to escort her and Travis out of Cassa di Molino. When he guided them past the bank president's outer offices, Kate searched for the woman from the ladies' room, but the dark-haired secretary wasn't at her desk.

Kate and Travis said goodbye to Maximo at the tall bronze doors guarding the entrance and stepped out into the bruising August sunshine. Heat slammed into her. Convinced the temperature had climbed ten or fifteen degrees during their extended lunch, she flung up a hand to block the shimmering, exhaust-fueled haze.

Which was why she didn't pick up on the drama occurring across the street as quickly as Travis did. She was still squinting through the exhaust fumes when she heard his smothered curse. Sensed him go rigid beside her. Caught a blur of movement as he burst into action.

Zigzagging across four lanes of traffic, he dodged a furiously honking driver and aimed for two figures locked in a desperate struggle. Kate was still standing openmouthed on the opposite side of the street when the two combatants turned to meet the unexpected attack. One, she saw with a shock, was the older woman from the bank. The other was a younger, wiry man wearing a striped soccer shirt and a look of vicious desperation.

Travis hit the male with a flying tackle. The woman

staggered back. A fist pressed to her bruised, bleeding mouth, she shouted something in Italian. Horrified, Kate picked up only one word.

Pistola.

"Travis!"

Heedless of traffic, she charged into the street.

"He's got a gun!"

She had to jump back to avoid being flattened by an oncoming bus. It was still rumbling by when a sharp crack split the hot, heavy air.

Chapter Fourteen

Kate's heart stopped dead in her chest. In the second or two it took for the bus to rumble by, she tried to convince herself that crack she'd heard was the sound of a backfire.

Please, let it be backfire!

A second, then a third sharp retort blasted that hope. Almost scorched by the searing exhaust from the tailpipe, she slapped a palm against the rear of the bus and cut around it.

The tableau on the sidewalk seemed to unfold before her horrified eyes like a video played in ultra slo-mo. The soccer-shirted punk was flat on the pavement. Travis had the kid's gun hand pinned to the sidewalk with one fist. His other was up and back and starting a vicious downward arc when the older woman threw herself at the two writhing combatants.

"No!" Her eyes wild, she grabbed Travis's wrist with both hands. *"E mio figlio!"*

Kate didn't try to translate the frantic cry. Her every thought, her entire being, was centered on the crimson splotch on Travis's shoulder. It blossomed even bigger and darker in the few desperate heartbeats it took her to reach the woman hanging on to him with clawing hands.

"E mio figlio! E mio figlio!"

Kate leaped at the dark-haired secretary, fully prepared to pulverize both her and the young tough with the gun. Travis kept his death grip on the punk's gun hand, but the unleashed energy went out of his upraised arm. He seemed to sag, his head down and his shoulders sloping. The momentary weakness combined with the spreading red stain struck terror into Kate's heart.

"Get off him!"

With a viciousness she didn't know she possessed, she grabbed the older woman's hair and yanked. The secretary yelped in pain and put both hands up to her temples. Remorseless, Kate hauled her away from the two men.

Only then did she realize a crowd had gathered. Other hands reached out to grab the older woman, to wrest the gun from the punk's hand, to help Travis roll off him and into a loose slump. Voices pounded at Kate. Questions bombarded her from all directions. Someone was shouting an urgent report into a cell phone.

The carabinieri who arrived on scene took Kate's name and disjointed statement and didn't protest when she insisted on climbing into the ambulance called to transport Travis to the hospital.

He was still in surgery when two other police officers arrived in the waiting room of the sprawling Saint Ursula-Malpighi University Hospital. They checked with the charge nurse and was told the bullet had passed through the victim's shoulder, causing as yet undetermined damage to muscle and the network of nerves running from his neck to his armpit. So Kate was less than sympathetic when the police sergeant confirmed what she'd already figured out for herself.

"The one who shoots your husband, he is the woman's son."

The lean, hard-eyed sergeant wore an olive-drab uniform crossed with a patent leather Sam Browne belt. Like Kate, he evinced little sympathy for the shooter.

"We know him well. He's... How do you say? Small-time. Too small to pay for the filth he pumps into his veins. He broke into his mother's house when she refuses to give him money." The sergeant's mouth twisted. "She also refuses to press charges."

Kate wasn't as forgiving. "Well, we will! This time," she vowed fiercely, "he's going down."

The sergeant nodded, took down her account of the event and promised he would have a translated copy ready for her signature when he returned to take Travis's.

"And these," he said, holding up a set of keys, "we recovered from the street. We've matched them to the car parked in the visitor's space at the bank, but this car is not yours."

Kate recognized the pawing black stallion on the key ring's medallion. "No, it belongs to a friend of ours. Maggiore Carlo di Lorenzo. He loaned it to my husband."

"So we have ascertained," the sergeant said, passing her the keys. "You have powerful friends, signora."

Kate nodded and dropped the keys in her pocket. Mere moments after the carabinieri departed, Signore Gallo and his assistant hurried into the surgical waiting area.

"Signora Westbrook!" The silver-maned bank executive grasped both of Kate's hands. "I cannot tell you how distressed we are that this should have happened."

"Signora Constanza is one of our most valued employees," Maximo put in. "She's been with Cassa di Molino for more than twenty years. But that son of hers. Pah!"

"The boy was such a bright child," Gallo said, shaking his head mournfully. "So happy. Gabriella—Signora Constanza—would bring him to the bank and we all delighted in his quick, eager mind." He sighed, and his expression folded into sorrowful lines. "Then came the drugs."

"Signore Gallo paid for him to go through rehab," Maximo related indignantly. "Not once, but twice! And still the *bastardo* bleeds his mother dry with desperate tales of how his suppliers will break his arm or shoot him in the knee or cut his throat. Better for Gabriella that they had!"

"Enough, Maximo. Let us focus instead on how we may assist Signora Westbrook in this unfortunate situation. Shall we arrange a place for you to stay while your husband recovers? A car and driver, perhaps, since you are unfamiliar with our city?"

"I have a car, but it's still parked in the visitor's space at the bank."

"Ah, yes. The red Ferrari. If you give me the keys, we shall deliver it here."

"Thank you."

"It is the least we can..."

He broke off, his glance whipping to the woman in surgical scrubs who pushed through the swinging doors. She removed her cap and released a short sweep of rich chestnut hair as her gaze landed on Kate.

"I am Dottore Bennati. You are Signora Westbrook?"

"Yes. How's my husband?"

"We have done debridement and *innesto di pelle*."

The surgeon searched for the medical terms in English and looked relieved when Signore Gallo offered to translate.

"She says they removed some damaged tissue and repaired an artery here." The banker tapped a spot close to his shoulder joint. "Luckily, the bullet was small caliber and did not fragment. It is too early to tell if it caused nerve damage, however."

"But my husband will be okay?"

"He will," Gallo confirmed after a brief colloquy with the ER doc. "Whether he will regain full use of his arm, however, must depend on the nerves."

Kate was so relieved by the first half of his comment that the second barely registered. "When can I see him?"

"Very soon," the banker translated. "He is in recovery now."

While Kate waited to see her husband, Signore Gallo assured her that Saint Ursula's School of Medicine and Surgery was the best in Italy and that Travis would recover speedily here. After repeating his offer of assistance, he and Maximo made sure Kate had their business cards and would call if she needed anything, anything at all.

The surgical recovery unit contained eight glassed-in cubicles in a neat semicircle around a central monitoring station. The gleaming floors and what looked like state-of-the-art equipment reassured Kate almost as much as Travis's wobbly smile when she entered his cubicle.

"Heya, Katydid."

His voice was thick, the words slurred. Kate dropped her purse on a chair and carefully threaded her hand through IV lines to take his.

"Heya, handsome. How do you feel?"

"Woozy, but flying high." He slicked his tongue across his lips and frowned in an obvious effort to clear the fog. "That kid? Wh-what happened to him?"

"He's in police custody."

"The woman?"

"She's his mother. He was trying to shake her down for drug money."

"Young…punk."

Kate's sentiments exactly, although she didn't voice them, as Travis's lids had drifted down. She sat there, his hand clasped loosely in hers, and tried not to relive those moments of sheer terror outside the bank.

An hour later Travis was moved to a single room overlooking a small garden. She stood by the window, waiting while the floor staff got him settled, took his vitals and adjusted his various drips and monitors. They were still entering information into a small, portable computer on a wheeled stand when Callie and Dawn arrived.

Callie eased past the nurses and wrapped an arm around Kate's shoulders before giving Travis a warm smile. "You don't look too bad for someone who got on the wrong side of a bullet."

Dawn just shook her head. "I thought you macho special ops types *knew* better than to get on the wrong side of a bullet."

"We do, most of the time. How did you two get here so quickly?"

"Carlo drove us. Carlo and Joe. Carlo had a night flight this evening, so they were just getting ready to head back to the base when Kate called."

"They'll be up in a minute," Callie related. "Joe's

parking the car, and Carlo detoured to speak to your surgeon."

The prince and his bodyguard arrived within moments of each other. Both were in flight suits, Carlo's with his velcroed name tag, wings and distinctive patches, Joe's with no markings at all. The prince repeated Signore Gallo's assurances that Saint Ursula's surgical unit was one of the top three in Italy and added that he'd personally verified Dr. Bennati's credentials.

"She is chairman of the department as well as surgeon in chief," he informed Travis. "You're lucky she was in the operating theater when they brought you in. And lucky, too," he added with a wiggle of his brows, "to have such a beautiful woman cutting on you, yes?"

His chauvinism was as cheerful as it was unabashed, although he attempted a quick recovery.

"But not as beautiful as the so lovely Dawn and Callie and Caterina."

"It's getting thick in here," Dawn commented drily. "And crowded. So these two so lovely ladies will wait in the lounge."

"It's a coffee bar," Callie told Kate. "Shall I bring you a cup?"

"No, I'll come down in a bit and get some."

She waited until she was sure Travis was comfortable with his visitors before slipping out to join her friends.

"What'd you do with Tommy?" she asked Dawn between much-needed sips.

"I called Brian right after you called us. He was already at the base but made immediate arrangements for one of the hotel staff to stay with Tom until he got back. He said they'd drive down to Bologna, too."

Kate wasn't sure Travis was up to a visit from both father and son. She also wondered what kind of memories of Italy Tommy would take home after so many visits to hospitals.

She needn't have worried on either count. By the time the Ellises arrived, Travis had improved enough to give a wide-eyed Tommy a much-expunged version of the shooting.

Carlo, thankfully, remained present when the police returned to take Travis's statement. Callie, Dawn, Joe and the Ellises retreated to the lounge during the process, which Kate guessed was considerably sped up by the prince's presence. When she tried later to express her appreciation for all Carlo had done, however, the prince merely shrugged.

"No thanks are necessary, Caterina. As I told you, I would be monkey bait were it not for your husband. Joe and I must go now, but we will return tomorrow. Also, I've reserved a hotel room for you and Callie, as she tells me she will stay in Bologna with you. And Dawn, if she…"

"Hold on." Brian strode into the room, trailed by Joe, Callie and Dawn, who had a close hold on Tommy. "I just got a call from our on-site rep. The NATO Evaluation Committee completed their review of the last three sortie results. They agree we've exceeded all test parameters. We've been green-lighted."

Carlo whooped and thumped his thigh with a fist. Travis's reaction was every bit as jubilant, if not quite as physical. Even Joe's habitually stony face broke into a satisfied grin.

"What does 'green-lighted' mean?" Dawn wanted to know.

"It means the mod Carlo and Travis and their crews have been testing did everything we advertised it would and more. EAS will go into full-scale development as soon as I get home."

"So you're finished at Aviano?"

"Pretty much." Brian gave his son's head a happy knuckle. "We'll fly back to the States next week, bud."

"But first we'll go to Rome 'n' see the Coliseum, right?"

"Right.

Tommy's whoop was much louder than the prince's and brought a nurse scurrying to check out the disturbance. After Carlo explained the situation in fluid Italian, she checked Travis's monitors and left with a gentle reminder that this *was* a hospital.

"The test crews will now disperse, as well," Carlo informed Dawn. "Mine will return to our base at Furbara, outside Rome. You must extend your stay and allow me to show you that most beautiful of all cities. You and Callie, of course."

"Of course," Callie murmured with a wry smile, but Dawn's glance went to Tommy before she answered.

"You're such a sweetie, Carlo, but I'm not sure what my plans are at this point. How about I contact you when I work them out?"

"Of course." The prince's dark eyes turned to Joe. "Our contract was for the duration of this special project, so I suppose you and your team will leave now, too."

"As soon as we get you back to Furbara and your own security detail takes over," he confirmed.

Kate couldn't help wondering why Carlo's personal security detail needed reactivating but knew better than to ask. The reason was no doubt shrouded by the same veil that had been draped over the rest of their highly classified project.

"Well, then," the prince proclaimed, "we must get

together a last time in Rome. All of us, yes? Assuming Travis is well enough to travel before we go our separate ways."

"I'll be well enough."

After everyone departed and the hospital had settled into the half-light of night, Kate shook out the sheets and blanket the nursing staff had thoughtfully provided. Frowning, Travis watched her tuck the sheets around the cushions of the reclining chair in the corner of his room.

"I still think you should have taken Carlo up on his offer of a hotel room for you and Callie."

"No way that was going to happen. Besides, Callie needed to drive back to Venice with Brian and Dawn to pack her things. We'll talk about a hotel room when she comes back down on the train tomorrow."

The chair made up, she edged it closer to his bed. Travis looked as though he wanted to continue arguing the point until she kicked off her shoes, curled up on the chair and slid her hand through the bed rails. His fingers twined with hers. For some moments the only sounds were the beep of the monitors and the occasional squeak of rubber soles in the hall.

Kate knew he had to be hurting, but he'd refused anything stronger than a mild painkiller. He'd also insisted the charge nurse use her handy-dandy portable computer to show him his electronic hospital record. He could read and interpret most of the numbers—temperature, pulse and respiratory rate, systolic blood pressure, oxygen saturation—but the surgical and postoperative notes required translation.

He rested more easily now, confident the wound wasn't disabling. She didn't want to burst his bubble but had to be honest.

"Dr. Bennati said the bullet went through your brachial...um..."

"Brachial plexus."

"Right. You could have nerve damage."

"I could. Don't think so, though."

She bit back a protest as he raised his injured arm a few cautious inches and lowered it just as carefully.

"Still have some range of motion. That's a good sign."

Maybe, but the effort had carved deep grooves at the corners of his mouth.

"Don't push it, okay? Dr. Bennati ordered a neurological consult. Let the experts do their thing."

"Nag, nag, nag."

"Ha! You want nagging, flyboy, you try getting out of bed before the docs and I say you can."

"I wouldn't have to, if you'd get in with me." His teasing grin faded, and he blew out a disgusted breath. "Helluva second honeymoon. I'd intended to do much better by you, Katydid."

"Are you kidding? Touring Italy in a red Ferrari? Gliding through Venetian canals in the moonlight? Curling up next to you in Saint Ursula's surgical ward? How much better can it get?"

"Oh, hell, the Ferrari. It's still parked at the bank."

"No, it's here. I gave Signore Gallo the keys and he had it delivered to the hospital."

"Gallo was here?"

"With Maximo. They showed up while you were still in surgery, both really devastated by the shooting. Evidently Signore Gallo's been trying to help the young thug you took down."

Kate shared what she knew, starting with the brief encounter with Gabriella in the ladies' room and ending with her son's failed attempts at rehab. Travis listened and made the appropriate noises at various points, but Kate could see the sad family tragedy didn't really engage him. What had, apparently, was Signore Gallo's interest in her career.

"He's taken quite a shine to you, Kate. Two meetings in less than a week. An elegant lunch. Putting you up for membership in that international association." The pillows whooshed air as he rested against them. His head angled, he looked at her through half-closed lids with eyes gone cool. "That should give your career a real boost."

Kate thought at first the pain had got to him. Just as quickly, she realized the problem wasn't physical.

Travis had jettisoned his military career for her. Correction, for them. Yet he'd walked out of the Cassa di Molino thinking she might take an appointment that would put her on a different continent at least once a quarter, possibly more often.

"Membership in the International Bankers' Association *could* give my career a boost," she agreed, "if I had any desire to accept it."

"You sounded pretty hyped about it this afternoon."

"I was surprised. And flattered," she admitted. "But as soon as I thought about it, I knew I wouldn't accept."

"Yet you told Gallo you'd think about it."

Whoa! Kate hadn't realized her starry-eyed reaction to the proposed nomination had cut so deep.

"The only reason I said I'd consider it was that I didn't want to throw what he considers a great honor back in his face."

She leaned against the bed rail, her hand still caught in Travis's.

"In fact, I've been thinking maybe I need to cut back

on my hours at the World Bank. Now that my husband's going to be hanging around the house a little more, I want some time with him. And with the baby I think we should start trying to make."

His lids lifted. The coolness melted, but the question that remained put a hurt in her heart.

"You sure about that, Kate? We've got a big change coming in our lives as it is. Think this is the right time to add another variable to the equation?"

"To hell with the equation. I'm done trying to calculate and assess and factor in every possibility in every situation."

"Good Lord! Did you feel that? I think the tectonic plates just shifted."

"I'm serious, dammit."

And she was. She was done with the uncertainty, the annoyance, the sheer stupidity of trying to reduce the unknown to a predetermined set of possibilities.

"No more spreadsheets," she promised fiercely. "No more eight-page itineraries or long lists of pros and cons. From now on we take every moment as it comes."

The smile was back, crinkling the tan lines at the corners of his eyes. "Oh, sweetheart, when we make a baby, we're going to need those spreadsheets and long lists. Especially if we have a Tommy the Terrible."

"Or a Tomasina the Terrible."

The prospect seemed to unman him, but he quickly recovered.

"Okay, I'm game. Let's go for it. But you'd better check and see if there's a lock on that door first."

"You idiot. I didn't mean we have to start working on the baby now."

"Why not?"

"Travis! You've been shot. And you're hooked up to all those monitors."

"So we give the nurses a thrill."

"Absolutely not." Her eyes misted, and a smile filled her heart. "But when we get you out of this bed, you're in for one helluva ride, flyboy!"

Chapter Fifteen

Kate, Travis, Callie and Dawn made the trip down from Bologna in comfort and luxury, courtesy of Carlo. Travis had his arm in a sling but had regained as much range of motion as he could manage without pulling stitches. The prognosis was for a full recovery, thank God.

The Ellises came in from Venice later that same afternoon. The prince had arranged accommodations for all of them at a five-star hotel on the Via Veneto, although all parties concerned insisted on paying for their rooms. That first evening they gathered for dinner at an outdoor restaurant highly recommended by the prince.

The following day was their last in Rome, and a surprised Kate was informed that Travis, Dawn and Callie had conspired to set the agenda. None of them would divulge all the details; they just told her to be ready to kick things off at 10:00 a.m. with a girls-only shopping expedition. She was ready as instructed but hated to leave Travis alone on the final day of their Roman holiday.

"Go," he insisted, his feet stretched out on a plush ottoman and the TV remote in hand. "ESPN is going to rebroadcast the UMass/UConn opening game of the season. I'll be fine."

"Fine, my ass," Dawn huffed. "You won't blink for the next three hours."

Which was pretty much what the doctor had ordered, Kate reminded herself. Still, she felt a little let down by his preference for football over a leisurely stroll through the gardens of the Villa Borghese or sitting in the sun on the Spanish Steps with a shared gelato.

"What about the others?" she asked as her friends shepherded her into a cab. "What's everyone doing today?"

"Brian's taking Tom to the Coliseum, Carlo's checking in at Furbara and Joe disappeared to take care of unspecified matters," Dawn related.

"I thought you wanted to take Tommy to the Coliseum."

"I did, but decided it would be better for them to have some guy time. I'll see enough of the kid when we get home."

"Come again?" Wedged in the cab's backseat between her two friends, Kate had to angle sideways to gape at a smug, smiling Dawn. "You're going to do it. Move in with the Ellises?"

"Just until Mrs. Wells is back on her feet."

"But...what about your job? Your apartment?"

"I emailed my boss and told him I'd be working from a remote location for a while. My apartment..." Her shoulders lifted in a careless shrug. "It'll still be there when I get back to Boston."

Kate slewed in the other direction. "Did you know about this?"

"Dawn discussed it with me this morning."

"And you think it's a good idea?"

A smile tugged at Callie's lips. "Better than jetting off to a resort in Marrakech for an indeterminate period, which is what Carlo is pressing her to do."

"Wow! Talk about choices."

Kate wanted to probe further, but the cab swerved onto a side street and rattled to a stop. She climbed out, then waited while Dawn paid the driver and Callie compared a handwritten address to that of the tiny boutique squeezed between a drugstore and a flower shop.

"This is the place," Callie confirmed.

Kate eyed the mannequin in the shop's narrow window dubiously. Bald and bent into a back-breaking contortion, it was draped in layers of violent color.

"You want to shop here?"

"We do," Dawn confirmed. "Carlo's cousin owns the shop."

"Of course."

"He says Stefania will have exactly what we're looking for."

"I'm not really looking for anything."

"Yes, you are. No way you're leaving Rome without one Italian designer original. Travis's orders," she added sternly when Kate started to protest. "Now come on and let Stefania show us her stuff."

Despite the tortured mannequin in the window, Stefania's stuff ran the gamut from ultra sleek to gorgeously soft and feminine. The elegant henna-haired shop owner had obviously been advised to expect them and had a selection waiting, all in Kate's size and chosen to match her coloring. Callie and Dawn settled into chairs while Kate performed a scene straight from *Pretty Woman.* Silks, linens, spandex, lace-trimmed leather... She modeled combinations in every color and fabric.

Cups of cappuccino appeared. Biscotti and almond fudge cookies *dis*appeared. Eyes narrowed, Stefania tapped a crimson-tipped nail against her cheek as her assistant adjusted the drape of a feather-trimmed tunic or repositioned a belt to ride lower on her customer's hips.

An hour later Kate had settled on a cloud-soft white silk dress with spaghetti straps and swirly hem cut on a sharp slant. A wide red leather belt, suitably adjusted to mirror the hem's angle, cost more than either the dress or the red-and-white polka-dot stilettos that Dawn insisted completed the look.

"Not quite," Callie said, smiling as she caught one side of Kate's hair back with a jaunty white fascinator à la the Duchess of Cambridge. "There. Perfect."

Kate twirled in the three-way mirror and had to agree. "Okay, I'm set. Now it's your turn."

"I don't need anything," Callie protested.

"Ha! That's what I said. But need it or not, I intend to buy something for you and Dawn. You've helped Travis and me so much these past few days. I..." She had to stop and swallow the lump that formed suddenly in her throat. "I don't know what I would have done without you."

"That's what friends are for," Dawn replied a little gruffly. "But if you insist on buying, I've been lusting after these wide-legged palazzo pants. And this blouse, Callie, is exactly the same shade of purple as your eyes."

They left the shop thirty minutes later. At Dawn's insistence, they wore their new finery to the next stop on the preplanned agenda. The busy salon was located on the Via Arcione and had also obviously been warned to expect them.

"Don't tell me," Kate said as the three women were whisked into chairs. "Carlo has another cousin in the beauty business."

"Nope. Joe recommended it."

Kate blinked. "As in big, strong, *silent* Joe Russo?"

"He's not so silent around our friend here," Dawn commented with a nod at Callie. "Don't know how she does it, but she always gets the male of the species talking."

"It's called listening," Callie said with unruffled calm. "Works every time."

Nails, toes and hair done, the three women exited the salon with their shopping bags and rumbling stomachs.

"I'm starved," Dawn announced. "Let's have lunch at some swanky restaurant."

Kate shook her newly washed and shiny hair. "Thanks, but I need to get back to the hotel and check on Travis."

"I bet he's so into that football game he doesn't even know you're gone."

"Probably, but I still want to head back."

"Okay but..."

"No *buts*, Dawn." Kate stepped to the curb to flag a cab. "I'm heading back."

"Could you give us five more minutes?"

The request came from Callie, who so rarely asked for favors that Kate dropped her arm.

"I guess. Why?"

"We're just around the corner from the Trevi Fountain. Your coin didn't go in last time. You can't leave Rome without another toss."

"You're right." Laughing, Kate hooked arms with her two friends. "Let's go do it."

The crowd at the tourist site was every bit as thick as it had been the first time they'd made the toss…except in one spot, Kate noted in surprise. Velvet ropes cleared a path down the steps, then right to the basin. And there, waiting at the fountain's rim, were four men. Four and a half, she amended as her startled gaze took in the boy grinning from ear to ear.

Travis wore his dress uniform, the sling fitted across his chest full of medals. Kate wondered for a dazed few seconds how he'd arranged to have it flown over from the States on such short notice. Then her glance shot to Carlo, whose dress uniform was even more resplendent. What looked like diamond-studded decorations filled a scarlet sash. And the hat tucked under his arm sported a matching plume!

Brian and Joe were in dark suits. Even Tommy wore a suit. Still stunned, Kate let her gaze drift from them to the avidly interested crowd to her two smiling friends.

"What is this?"

"It was Travis's idea," Callie said. "He told us he planned to ask you to renew your wedding vows while you were in Italy."

"We suggested the Trevi Fountain," Dawn continued with a grin. "Then sweetie pie Carlo stepped in to take charge, and here we are."

"And here we are," Kate echoed, touched and almost overwhelmed.

"Here, I'll take those."

Dawn grabbed the shopping bags and nudged Kate onto the velvet-roped path. She understood the new dress and shoes now, even the fascinator. She felt every bit as glamorous as the Duchess of Cambridge as she floated down the steps and glided toward her husband.

Hundreds of cell phone cameras clicked and whirred. Grinning kids in backpacks wedged close to tourists in fanny packs to get a shot of the star attraction. Kate caught comments in a half dozen languages, probably everyone asking who the heck she was.

Then the crowd and the chatter and the clicking faded, and there was only Travis stepping forward. She felt the strength in the hand he held out to her, heard the love in his murmured "Hello, Katydid."

And saw the promise of forever in his smile.

* * * * *

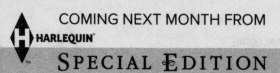

COMING NEXT MONTH FROM

SPECIAL EDITION

Available March 22, 2016

#2467 FORTUNE'S SPECIAL DELIVERY
The Fortunes of Texas: All Fortune's Children
by Michelle Major
British playboy Charles Fortune Chesterfield doesn't think he'll ever settle down. That is, until he runs into a former girlfriend, Alice Meyers, whose adorable baby looks an awful lot like him...

#2468 TWO DOCTORS & A BABY
Those Engaging Garretts!
by Brenda Harlen
Dr. Avery Wallace knows that an unplanned pregnancy will present her with many challenges—but falling in love with Justin Garrett, her baby's father, might be the biggest one of all!

#2469 HOW TO LAND HER LAWMAN
The Bachelors of Blackwater Lake
by Teresa Southwick
April Kennedy is tired of being the girl Will Fletcher left behind. When he fills in as the town sheriff for the summer, she plans to make him fall for her, then dump him. But Cupid has other plans for them both.

#2470 THE COWBOY'S DOUBLE TROUBLE
Brighton Valley Cowboys
by Judy Duarte
When rancher Braden Rayburn finds himself looking after orphaned twins, he hires a temporary nanny, Elena Ramirez. He couldn't ever imagine they would fall for the kids—and each other—and create the perfect family.

#2471 AN OFFICER AND HER GENTLEMAN
Peach Leaf, Texas
by Amy Woods
Army medic Avery Abbott is suffering from severe PTSD—and she needs assistance, stat! Thanks to dog trainer Isaac Meyer and Avery's rescue pup, Foggy, Avery may have found the healing she requires—and true love.

#2472 THE GIRL HE LEFT BEHIND
The Crandall Lake Chronicles
by Patricia Kay
When Adam Crenshaw returns to Crandall Lake, Eve Kelly can't help but wonder if she should've let the one who got away go. And she's got a secret—her twins belong to Adam, her first love, and so does her heart...

"Thank you for tonight," she said as she walked him to
the door. "I was planning on leftovers when I got home—
this was better."

"I thought so, too." He settled his hands on her hips
and drew her toward him.

She put her hands on his chest, determined to hold him
at a distance. "What are you doing?"

"I'm going to kiss you goodbye."

"No, you're not," she said, a slight note of panic in
her voice.

"It's just a kiss, Avery." He held her gaze as his hand
slid up her back to the nape of her neck. "And hardly our
first."

Then he lowered his head slowly, the focused
intensity of those green eyes holding her captive as his
mouth settled on hers. Warm and firm and deliciously

intoxicating. Her own eyes drifted shut as a soft sigh whispered between her lips.

He kept the kiss gentle, patiently coaxing a response. She wanted to resist, but she had no defenses against the masterful seduction of his mouth. She arched against him, opened for him. And the first touch of his tongue to hers was like a lighted match to a candle wick—suddenly she was on fire, burning with desire.

It was like New Year's Eve all over again, but this time she didn't even have the excuse of adrenaline pulsing through her system. This time, it was all about Justin.

Or maybe it was the pregnancy.

Yes, that made sense. Her system was flooded with hormones as a result of the pregnancy, a common side effect of which was increased arousal. It wasn't that she was pathetically weak or even that he was so temptingly irresistible. It wasn't about Justin at all—it was a basic chemical reaction that was overriding her common sense and self-respect. Because even though she knew that he was wrong for her in so many ways, being with him, being in his arms, felt so right.

Don't miss
TWO DOCTORS & A BABY
by Brenda Harlen,
available April 2016 wherever
Harlequin® Special Edition books and ebooks are sold.

www.Harlequin.com

THE WORLD IS BETTER WITH

Romance

Harlequin has everything from contemporary, passionate and heartwarming to suspenseful and inspirational stories.

Whatever your mood, we have a romance just for you!

Connect with us to find your next great read, special offers and more.

f /HarlequinBooks

🐦 @HarlequinBooks

www.HarlequinBlog.com

www.Harlequin.com/Newsletters

⬧HARLEQUIN®

A *Romance* FOR EVERY MOOD™

www.Harlequin.com